Children
of
FINA

Children
of
FINA

GABRIEL ANTHONY LOPEZ

Printed in the United States of America
ISBN 978-1-64133-939-1 (sc)
ISBN 978-1-64133-940-7 (e)
ISBN 978-1-64133-941-4 (hc)

2024.10.01

This book is printed on acid-free paper.

Because of the dynamic nature of the Internet, any web addresses or links contained in this book may have changed since publication and may no longer be valid. The views expressed in this work are solely those of the author and do not necessarily reflect the views of the publisher, and the publisher hereby disclaims any responsibility for them.

Blue Ink Media Solutions
1111B S Governors Ave
STE 7582 Dover,
DE 19904

www.blueinkmediasolutions.com

Children *of* Fina

I

He's talking about Kernanites. Kernanites are everywhere. And Atticus Lokar was the center of attention. He was at the bar.

"I like life," said Atticus to the bartender. "People who do not make it. And alcohol has a place throughout history."

The bartender winked.

"I know your mother died recently during the pandemic," he said as he cleaned more whiskey glasses with a towel.

Atticus was thinking of something better to say to the bartender.

"What's your name? he asked.

"Hank," said the bartender rather curtly.

"We need to break the ice, Hank," said Atticus, "Since most people just lost someone in a pandemic and throughout the solar system, we are losing our touch, our magic."

"I was just thinking outside the box a little when I commented about your mother," said Hank. "How did everything work out genetically during the pandemic? Is that what you wanted for your mother to die?" said Hank.

"That was a random statement. Who cares about these days," said Atticus. "Could I have another drink?"

Atticus' friends buzzed freely around him as he talked to Hank. To consume oneself with alcohol and friends can be great but also oppressive. Atticus took note of the bartenders' words, but the suddenness of being thrown into an apocalypse made dancing and drinking enticing. He did not care what other people were thinking now. Nor did he care what other people said there were better people than him, or he was in an imposter. He wanted to live in the *now*, an intoxicating now. Not minding the crowd in the bar, Atticus threw a dart across the room and hit the bull's eye. Atticus looked around the room to see if he could find a dance partner. His other duties were in the back of his mind. Some male bar patrons danced enthusiastically.

Atticus stumbled across a couple of tables and landed at a table occupied by an older man. The older man was in a uniform from the Star Union. He looked at Atticus with stern, caring eyes. Atticus stared back at him.

"Do you need any more?" he said. "I think you've had enough and could learn a thing or two." The older man uncrossed his arms and placed a Star Union medal on Atticus' chest. Atticus let out a small moan and said, "Thank you, sir."

Atticus lay on his back and grabbed the medal. He sat up and gazed around the bar. Next to him was a glass containing a Long Island Iced Tea, and he took a swig of it. Everyone in the bar continued their raucous behavior.

Suddenly, the power went out in the bar. The music stopped, and Atticus was forced to confront the older man, who sneered.

"So, were you ever in battle?" said Atticus.

"Yes, I was. On the Corniz front," said the old man, politely sipping his drink.

"Wasn't that front fought well," said Atticus.

"We decimated the enemy but lost a lot of fighters," said the old man, pointing at a scar on his face.

"I heard the stories growing up," said Atticus. "Sorry, I did not catch your name?" "I'm Captain Reno Bahm," said Bahm.'

"I have heard the name," said Atticus.

"The war hero who joined the other side," said Atticus. "Your actions taught us all a lesson. You can't trust Kernanites."

"We should go up to the atrium," said the captain.

Atticus looked around the bar. The bar was still thick, with people partying. He took one last shot of alcohol and headed in the direction the captain was going to.

"So, tell me about the Battle of Corniz," said Atticus.

"There were long, hard, brutal days. We were on the planet Stogh. Every city was razed," said Captain Bahm. "We fought back from the wilderness. They took all the cities."

Both were walking to the atrium as fireworks were seen through the skylight. On the planet Fina, there was always a party. Brahm looked like he was battle-hardened, and Atticus wanted to ask the question again about what would bring him to Fina.

"So, what brought you out to Fina," said Atticus.

"I left the Star Union after the war was over with the Kernanites. I was looking for some peace and comfort," said Brahm.

"Same," said Atticus. "The war brought disease, and when the pandemic broke out, I lost my mother. I lost my father long ago in a forgotten war.

"Where are you from?" said Captain Bahm.

"I'm from Stie Lux," said Atticus.

"An Independent World. That's nice," said Captain Bahm. "Fina has been good to me. Nice people and atmosphere. But I've been searching for something."

Atticus furrowed his brow. He had always been taken as the searcher among his crew of friends. An older man still searching puzzled him.

"I've seen some things and perhaps too much," said Captain Bahm. "When the Kernanites took my world, I only wanted to battle and get revenge."

"How did revenge leave you feeling since the Kernanites were once one with our people," said Atticus.

Atticus never had seen a Kernanite. They were invisible to him. He never thought fighting such an invisible enemy was worth it, given you cannot see them. He liked things fair and just. His people, the Independents, had a different view of the Kernanites. A misunderstood enemy was trounced upon by the Star Union when the Star Union started colonizing planets close to them. The term "Kernanites" was more of a nickname. People have heard their language, and it is rumored that they call themselves something different. The nickname came from their fantastic display of technology, advancement, and skill in war.

"I came to you, Atticus because I need help from the Independents," said Captain Bahm.

"Why? Sorry for being a little blunt," said Atticus.

"The Kernanites plan to attack more worlds going past the boundary we set when we colonized the planets near them," said Captain Bahm.

"I have a connection to some remote planets," said Atticus.

"Which ones?" said Captain Bahm.

"Ure and Tenament II," said Atticus.

"Those are remote but well-known planets," said Captain Bahm.

Captain Bahm's battle-scared face looked relaxed and pleasant as he took in the destinations Atticus named. Atticus put his feet up on the table. He called a waiter over to the table. Captain Bahm was sitting at the bar and brought out a star map. He set it on the table. Bahm looked over the map and picked Ur and Tenament II.

"I need ore and a new ship," said Atticus.

Atticus considered Bahm's request. He had been lying low on Fina for some time. He did not want to get called into service even by the Independents. He thought about the cost. Looking out across the bar, he spotted the waitress, and she spotted him. She walked over and set down a napkin on the table.

"What can I do for you two guys," said the waitress. She was a Humar. Atticus pondered who he was about to talk to now. Humar's were rare to see. They had become hermits for the past fifty years with the wars. Her crystal skin glistened in the bar light.

"I want two Rael beers," said Atticus.

"Rael!" said the waitress. "Are you having a celebration?"

"Yes, I am celebrating my new acquaintance, Captain Reno Bahm," said Atticus.

Atticus nudged Bahm because he was about to compliment a Humar. Her green eyes stood out from her crystal-white skin. She stood there briefly analyzing Bham and Atticus.

The Humar quickly turned her back to order the beers. She sifted through the crowd until she reached the cooking and drinking area. Atticus thought she was beautiful and wanted to ask her name.

She walked back over and handed the two their beers.

"What's your name?" said Atticus as he placed his hand on hers.

She immediately blushed and laughed. Her crystal-white skin changed to fluorescent pink to indicate her mood, and she liked what was happening. At least, that was how Atticus understood the display of emotion.

"Sorry, I'm owned," said the Humar. "But my name is Aida for future reference. And you may need it."

Atticus thought slavery had been abandoned on Fina long ago, but it did not seem wholly. Atticus looked at her body for malnourishment and abuse. He found none.

"Slavery was banned on Fina long ago. Who are you owned by?" said Atticus.

"You don't know who the real master here is on Fina. The Protector is the real master of this world," she cooed.

"Who is that?" said Atticus.

Bahm looked at him and gave Atticus a sign to quit talking to the Humar. Things were getting exciting tonight for Atticus. *Someone from the Star Union, a Humar, what next could happen?*

"Look, Atticus," said Bahm. He pointed towards the bar's doorway and past the crowds of people. A group of Itors were walking into the bar. Itors were also rare these days. They also secluded themselves when the war with the Kernanites broke out in the galaxy.

"Itors!" said the Humar. "Sorry, got to go, more patrons."

Atticus calculated what he could gain by an encounter with Itors. Itors were nefarious. They were called everything by the outside world: swindlers, charlatans, and cons. Their home planet was Vinosa. Bham started to ask for more Rael beer. Atticus watched as the Itors walked over to the bar and then to the direction of their table.

Atticus guessed right that he was going to have an encounter with Itors. They sniffed the air and belched. The first Itor seemed to be their leader. The other two were sidekicks.

"You Stie Luxian!" said the first Itor, who had black and yellow skin. "Are you genetically engineered?"

"I am fully Stie Luxian. No genetic modifications. Who is asking?" said Atticus.

"King Kuckgo of the Utopian Nebula!" touted the Itor.

"I have never heard of such a person. I have heard of someone call the Protector here on Fina," asserted Atticus.

"Would he be of any use to Itors of every race," said the Itor. "We have worked hard to reach the Utopian Nebula before, the birth of worlds and stars."

Bahm brought Atticus to the side. He looked confused. He motioned to the door.

"I thought you were going to help me get to the Independent Worlds," said Bahm.

"Well, I decided to inquire more about what Fina was about. I have lived here most of my life without any action or information," said Atticus.

The Itors went to the front of the bar and requested a translator. Atticus saw Aida talking to them and the bar's owner. Aida headed in Atticus' direction, and she waved back as Atticus looked directly at them. The Itors plodded over with their big, muscular builds.

"You Stie Luxian! What is your name?" said the first Itor.

"My name is Atticus Lokar of Stie Lux; it's a pleasure to meet you," said Atticus with a grin.

"You can provide us with safe passage to an Independent world?" said the first Itor.

"First, what's your name so we can gain familiarity."

"My name is Llub, and this is Rotris and Yeys," said Llub, pointing to his associates.

Atticus analyzed the Itors. They also did not seem a threat but could cause trouble if they started talking to Bahm. Itors did not like the wars and were usually gregarious, joyful races with intimidating looks.

Bahm pulled Atticus aside again. Sweat started to percolate on his brow. He also clenched his jaw.

"You know Atticus Itors did not like this war, or any war for that matter," said Bahm. "You have a debt to pay for agreeing to take me to the Independent Worlds."

"I can handle this, Bahm. It may seem I am shaking off debt, but I am not. I am thinking ahead," said Atticus.

Itors also had above-average galactic ships equipped with weapons and the latest propulsion. The Itors grew temperamental and huffed at Atticus and Bahm. They were known for displays of emotions, as were the Humar.

Atticus felt intimidated for a second. Aida entered the situation. She looked at Atticus, Itors, and Bahm. She opened her hands and approached the Itors with palms facing up in a gesture of peace.

"You mean no harm, Humar?" said Llub. "I hear otherwise in the galaxy. There are plenty of stories of Humar's becoming too opportunistic and treacherous."

"I am on my own in this galaxy now. I abandoned my people for the adventure of the galaxy; I make my way; I am the property of the Protector here on Fina, though."

"What does that mean—The Protector," said Llub.

"He unites all and resides in Epkhaliz City on the Zernog continent," said the Humar.

"We wish to bypass this Protector," said Llub. The other Itors grunted in agreement. Saliva dripping from their mouths. Aida talked to the Itors for a bit longer, and Bahm and Atticus watched as she expressed herself in multiple languages other than her own. Bahm breathed a sigh of relief.

"Things seem to be going well with the Itors, but I need an introduction," he said.

Atticus motioned over to Aida. She came over and placed her hands on her hips. She took a swig of his beer.

"What do you say when introducing Bahm?" said Atticus.

"I'm for it. It looks like you cannot keep the guy a secret," she said.

"He's ex-military from the Star Union, though."

"Just a bad reputation, the war got him. Fina and the Protector is the healer of all problems," said Aida.

"Would they think about what they said after I talked to them? They look like they'll be up for anything," said Aida.

"I'll introduce myself," said Bahm.

"Suit yourself," said Aida.

"Hello, Llub and associates. I am Captain Reno Bahm from the Star Union. It's a pleasure to meet you, and I am also looking for a way to the Independent Worlds."

"You are from the Star Union?" Llub chuckled. "It's the same with them. There are so many rumors of a change with them. Although Itors have highly appreciated their level-headedness for the past half-decade."

"So, you do not consider me a threat or an asset to trade on the slave market," said Bahm.

"None!" shouted Llub, "What we need is safe passage to the Independent Worlds as soon as possible."

Bahm was stunned at how demanding the Itors were in front of him. Atticus was weary of their character shifts as well. Atticus took a swig of his beer.

"Now that we got the safety concern out of the way," said Atticus.

Bahm looked at them smugly. The Itors began to grunt in excitement. They brought out the star maps as they were agreeing.

"Then it is a deal," said Llub, "We'll head to the Independent Worlds."

By this time, the lights in the bar had started to turn off, and the crowds were thinning. The Itors shook hands with Bahm and Atticus. Aida grabbed their things and headed their way.

II

Atticus woke up in a Star Jumper. Fields of stars zipped past him as he awoke from a long sleep. Aida slept across from him. They were traveling to the Independent Worlds, a map stipulated. Bahm was in the pilot seat. And the Itors were also sleeping in the back. Atticus went and sat next to Bahm in the co-pilot's chair.

"How's the flying so far?" said Atticus as he further shook off the effects of sleep.

"It's going well," managed Bahm. The need for sleep appeared on his face. Atticus took note of it.

"When was the last time you got some sleep," inquired Atticus. A ping sound emitted from the Star Jumper's operations console. Atticus and Bahm brushed it aside to keep them on track to the Independent Worlds.

"Where are we at right now?" petitioned Atticus.

"We are about to go through the Utopian Nebula," stated Bahm.

The ping from the operation's console on the Star Jumper continued to emit, and then more pinging came from the science console. Bahm looked irritated. Atticus looked around the consoles.

"Do we veer from our path to inquire what may be out there?" said Atticus.

"Does it look like it is following us?" said Bahm.

Atticus looked over all the consoles. He went to the science station where he could scan where the pings were coming from and determine if they were a threat. He could hear the Itors awaken in the back of the Star Jumper.

"The results are inconclusive whether or not it is following us, but it does appear non-threatening," concluded Atticus as he sighed in relief. Atticus could only imagine the sun's warmth touching his skin on Fina as he walked through the fields. He missed home more than he could express.

Atticus looked through more data, transmissions, and signals from the pings on their scanner. Bahm and Atticus wanted to pass through the Utopian Nebula safely so they would not encounter allies of the Kernanites.

"Hey! Hey!" said Aida and Bahm to Atticus.

Atticus whirled around as he stood over the consoles. The darkness of space made Aida's skin glisten even more, and Atticus wondered what it would look like beneath the sun of his home world, Stie Lux. Her eyes were bright and curious after sleep.

"Aida, how did you get into the front section of the Star Jumper?" said Atticus.

"Every good person from Fina has learned how to access doors and pick ancient locks," mocked Aida.

Atticus puffed up and swallowed his pride that he may be falling in love with this female, a formerly enslaved person. Right now, he was more concerned about the pings, and he truly wanted Aida out of the ship's command center and the pilot's section. Atticus sighed.

"Now, go back to sleep or grab some food," said Atticus.

"What are those sounds?" said Aida

"It's the scanners picking up objects in space," stated Attiucs.

Aida peered intensely at the screens. Atticus felt the intensity of her gaze. He thought there was more to Aida than she told him. Something truly remarkable.

An alarm sounded in the command center. Atticus stood attentively, and Aida approached the consoles. Atticus' eyes jumped from screen to screen. What he saw made him glad he was on a Star Jumper.

"What's out there?" inquired Bahm.

"It seems we got some incoming friends," Atticus sarcastically states.

"Thank you, but no, thank you for your sarcasm," Aida snarled.

Aida crossed her arms and leaned against the wall of the Star Jumper. She began to listen to the instructions and commands Atticus was given to Bahm. These were humanoids doing typical humanoid things in this situation.

"Maybe I can help?" said Aida.

Atticus shooed Aida into the passenger module of the Star Jumper. He sat down at the co-pilot's chair to tell Bahm the latest about the objects they were picking up approaching them. Atticus noticed Bahm's hands were shaking.

"Do you know where you are?" questioned Atticus.

"We are near the Utopian Nebula heading towards the Independent Worlds," anxiously answered Bahm. His eyes bounced from instrument to instrument in front of him. Atticus looked out at the distant colors of the nebula.

The Star Jumper rocked suddenly. Aida let out a scream of surprise, and the Itors roared awake and shouted questions about the condition of the Star Jumper. Atticus hurried over to the science and operations console.

"An ion canon has struck us," said Atticus, "We took hits on levels 3, 4, and 5 and the cargo area. We're still holding steady!"

"Who opened fire?" said Bahm.

"I'm trying to identify them," said Atticus.

"They look like Crinix Imperial fighters," said Atticus bravely.

"What are they doing out here," said Bahm.

"I've heard the Crinix Imperium has been swaying towards the side of the Kernanites from the consequences of the war," added Aida.

"I'll try to open up a communication link with them," said Atticus.

The Star Jumper rocked violently again. Aida accidentally clung to Atticus. He looked quizzically at her.

"Does it look like they're backing off?" demanded Bahm.

"No, it doesn't," stated Atticus, "So, it looks like we have a fight on our hands, or we need to try to shake them off."

"We'll be inside the Utopian Nebula in about 15 clicks," said Bahm.

Bright flashes of light whizzed past the Star Jumper. Bahm began attempting to shake off the Crinix Imperial fighters. Aida went into the passenger module.

"Nothing to see here, Llub," said Aida as the Itor approached the command center.

"What is going on? Are we taking enemy fire?" said Llub.

"You could say that, but it's all been sorted out. We'll be inside the nebula in 15 clicks," comforted Atticus.

Llub did not look convinced. He then looked at Aida intensely. Then he let a grunt.

"You, Humar," he said, "You have special powers. Now would be a good time to use them."

"I have special powers, maybe, but no need to rush," taunted Aida.

"I'm punching it towards the nebula," said Bahm.

As they felt the propulsion jettison them into the nebula, the Star Jumper spun out of control and stopped just inside the nebula. Atticus and Aida landed on the floor. And Llub was thrown back into the passenger section. Bahm was still safely in his seat.

"What just happened?" said Bahm.

Atticus quickly got up and looked at the operations and science consoles. Aida also got up and went to where Atticus stood in the command module. Llub made his way back to the command center.

"It looks like they hit us with some grappling hook," said Atticus.

"Can we shake it off?" said Bahm.

"Yes, we can, but we need some kind of external force to put on it to break free," said Atticus.

"The Humar should help," said Llub.

"Stop bringing up my so-called special powers, or you could start to experience some Llub," said Aida.

Atticus clenched his jaw. *Could Aida help, though?* Atticus inputted some data and drew up some calculations.

"So, could you help us, Aida," demanded Atticus.

"I guess I could," Adia said in a shaky tone. She grew nervous, showing her special skills.

She was not always asked to use her telekinesis.

"What can I help with, Aida?" said Bahm.

"Try propelling the Star Jumper, but still let the grappler have slack," said Aida.

Aida went to the operations and science stations. She looked at a digital screen showing the grappling hook. She needed a specific location, so she also found the coordinates of the Crinix Imperial fighters.

Captain Bahm sped up the Star Jumper. As soon as it halted, Aida closed her eyes and spoke words Atticus and Lullb could not hear.

Sounds of metal grinding and popping filled the air. Bahm looked at some sensors, which showed that the grappling hook was starting to give way. Aida pressed her hand against her temple and touched the operations and science stations.

"Almost there," exclaimed Bahm.

Aida started to look exasperated, but suddenly, the Star Jumper lurched forward and spun further into the nebula, losing the Crinix Imperial fighters. Bahm took some time to get the Star Jumper to orient itself correctly. Everyone checked their consoles and sensors to see if the Crinix Imperial fighters were still there.

"Impressed?" suggests Aida to Atticus.

"I am a bit impressed," cringed Atticus, "I never knew a Humar had so much fight in her."

"Well, we're not all mysterious star hoppers of the galaxy," stated Aida.

"We should continue our way to King Kuckgo of this nebula," grunted Llub. "We need safer passage since allies of Kernanites caught our trail."

"I agree with Llub," said Bahm.

"We need to send a probe to alert them that we are heading in their direction," said Llub.

Atticus looked at his console. This Star Jumper only had two. He looked at how much fuel they had and selected the first one. The Star Jumper lurched as the probe was jettisoned. Captain Bahm started the engines of the Star Jumper and went in the direction of the probe.

The rest of the Itors were around a table eating. Their grunts and huffiness were heard throughout the Star Jumper. Aida, Atticus, and Llub were sitting next to them, thinking what they should do next now that enemies had spotted them.

"Do you think King Kuckgo will still take us in and harbor us for a while?" said Aida.

"It is hard to know now. Whoever ratted on our coordinates is an enemy indeed," said Llub.

Atticus kept his head low and thought about all his experiences in the other worlds, especially now that they were heading back to the Independent Worlds. He looked over at Aida; from what Atticus could gather, she would soon no longer be enslaved. Llub and the others were ready for their destination. Atticus went back up to the command module.

"What do we go on the sensors?" Atticus stated to Bahm.

"We have some debris coming in back other than that. It's OK," comforted Bham.

"Where is the debris from?" inquired Atticus.

"It seems it is from an old shipyard in the nebula," said Bahm

"Anything in there we could use," said Atticus.

"Glad you asked because we barely have to adjust our course to reach it. We'll still be on schedule," commanded Bahm.

As Atticus looked out the command module's windows, he could see the remnants of thousands of ships. Some dating back to a time before the unification of the known worlds. He was hoping to find some fuel.

"Where can we land?" demanded Atticus.

"There is no place to land. You will have to approach with a spacesuit to where our sensors are pointing too," chimed Bahm.

"We're looking for fuel!" Atticus said to everyone. "Does anyone want to take a detour?"

A few of the Itors raised their hands. Llub was one. Atticus looked at Aida, and she just winked at him.

"Okay, we need to get our suits on and ensure everyone stays in communication," ordered Atticus.

Atticus looked at a computer, and then some data went into a tablet lying on the console. The computer had found several places where fuel signatures had been found. They all lined up at the bottom of the Star Jumper to perform some spacewalking.

Atticus had only been propelled through space with a suit once before, and it startled him at how easily the task could go awry. Lullb and two other Itors looked puffed up in their suits. They remained quiet.

"1, 2, 3…. Go!" screamed Atticus.

He opened the door to the outside, and Atticus and the Itors were pushed out of the Star Jumper because of decompression. They zoomed through the length of a battlecruiser to the shipyard below the Star Jumper. Atticus and the Itors brought out their sensor devices. They found a civilian vessel, and it looked like it still had large amounts of fuel stored.

"Let's hit the civilian cruiser," communicated Atticus.

The Itors got in the back of him as they lined up to land on the cruiser. Atticus and the Itors readied their gravity boots. As soon as they came within running distance of the cruiser, the gravity boots attached to the metal of the cruiser. Atticus was breathing with suspense, and so were the Itors.

"How was that?" he said.

"It was a joy ride! Isn't that what you Stie Luxians call it," said Llub.

"Not quite," Atticus said politely while holding his head and hitting the communication button.

"So, we need the easiest door, escape hatch, or cargo hold," said Atticus.

"I'm picking up where the fuel is. Some of it is in a cargo hold about 50 rumas from here," said one of the Itors.

Atticus got the directions from the Itors and headed in the direction the sensors said the fuel was in. When they got to the cargo hold, Atticus plugged some numbers into the computer on his wrist. The wrist on his computer opened up the cargo hold. A forcefield was still in place. Atticus did more scanning. They found an entry point.

"Over here! I found an entry point where we can enter the cruiser without fear of decompression," Atticus commanded.

The Itors acknowledged and followed Atticus. They reached the entry point and went through pressurization to enter the cruiser. Some of the lights flickered on and off at the entry point. Atticus touched a door with his wrist computer.

"The sensors detected the fuel just ahead," said Atticus.

When they reached the cargo hold, it was dark. Atticus and the Itor's pulses elevated. Atticus returned the medical information to the Star Jumper if they needed assistance. One of the Itors hesitated.

"Something is not right," said the Itor. Itors were known to have great senses, so Atticus trusted him. Llub and Atticus grabbed a light stick from their suits. They showed the light around the cargo hold.

"What is it? What happened here?" said Llub in a worried voice. And, Itors do generally not worry. Atticus took some more steps forward. What Atticus found frightened him.

"These are dead soldiers from the Star Union," Atticus said in a voice of shock. He ran the lightstick over their bodies. There were eleven bodies he counted.

"Do you think they were a crew?" said Atticus to Llub.

"There is no way to know, but it is unusual that we would find death in the Utopian Nebula," said LLub.

Whoever did this to these soldiers thought Atticus and the others must have something against the Star Union. He immediately thought of their safety. Captain Bahm was a former soldier and captain in the Star Union. Atticus immediately tapped his communication device to speak to Bahm.

III

Blood stained the clothes of the dead soldiers found on the civilian cruiser. Llub, Atticus, and the other Itors took a more complex look around the cargo hold. Ion guns seemed to have been shot on both sides of the room. An Itor grabbed something that looked like an identification badge from one of the fallen soldiers.

"These are no ordinary soldiers. They are special operations soldiers," affirmed the Itor.

Atticus had not received a message from Captain Bahm, so he decided to scan the area to send holographic data. The civilian cruiser jolted suddenly. The eerie sounds of the stressed hull giving in filled the room. The cruiser was also lacking proper shielding.

"I suggest we go back to the Star Jumper," ordered Atticus, "We can access more information from the soldiers' badges. We will go back the way we came into the cruiser."

"What about the fuel?" said Llub.

"We can decompress the cargo hold and tag the fuel cells. They will float out into space, and we can pick up the fuel cells robotically from the Star Jumper," suggested Atticus.

"That sounds good," said Llub.

The other Itors made their way back inside the battle cruiser. Atticus and Llub did as well. They first ensured the fuel cells were expelled from the cruiser when they reached the entrance. They were back in the Star Jumper in no time. And, with the help of Atticus, Captain Bahm could gather the fuel cells.

Tensions were high between Atticus and Bahm. Bahm knew nothing of what they had found, but the special operations soldiers seemed to have been looking for something. Atticus grew nervous as he thought about the dead soldiers he encountered. He was glad he was from the Independent Worlds, and his people did not like violence.

"Find anything?" said Aida.

"Nothing, just fuel," asserted Atticus.

The Itors were tired from the mission to the cruiser. They searched the Star Jumper for more food. Atticus went to the command module, and Bahm retook a seat in the pilot's chair.

"So, where are we headed to Atticus," questioned Bahm.

"In the direction of the probe and the King Kuckgo's planet," said Atticus.

"Excellent. We have fuel and nobody on our trail," said Bahm.

Atticus laughed nervously as he pushed the soldiers' images out of his mind. He knew Captain Bahm was a decorated military man who had also done special operation missions. Everything would make sense again once they reached King Kuckgo.

Captain Bahm charged the engines, and they zoomed off through the nebula again. The Itors and Aidia fell asleep again. Atticus sat in the chair next to Captain Bahm so that they could alternate piloting duties. *The Itors would never tell what they found on the cruiser, would they?* After two or three shifts piloting, Atticus got tired of piloting and returned to the science and operation modules to see how close they had gotten to King Kuckgo's planet of Jeolt.

The probe reached the Star Jumper before arriving at Jeolt. Atticus was in the cargo hold of the Star Jumper, looking over the probe and downloading data. He spent several hours searching for more information about the Kernanites and their allies following them, but no information surfaced.

The nebula and its colors mashed with one another and continued to fly past the windows of the Star Jumper. They were still in hyperdrive. Jeolt was within range of their sensors. Atticus was still bothered by the dead soldiers on the civilian cruiser. They were looking for something, but what he did not know.

Atticus was finishing up with the probe when the Star Jumper dropped out of hyperspace. Green clouds swirled over the yellow and brown continents of Jeolt, and a purple sea welcomed them. Several Jeoltian fighter craft started to guide the Star Jumper to a spaceport.

The Star Jumper docked, and everyone instantly looked more relaxed. Bahm got out of the pilot's chair, Atticus followed, and the others patiently waited for the crew to leave the Star Jumper.

At the space dock, they found translators, and their home worlds were recognized with their identification badges. They requested to see King Kuckgo. An ambassador appeared before them in a waiting area.

"Friends," he said, "You've requested to meet King Kuckgo. This is a high demand. Do you mind if I ask why?"

Atticus stuck out his hand and said, "Hello, I am Atticus Lokar from Stie Lux. Meeting you and being amongst the king's subjects is a pleasure. We have had a request for safety here for a while."

The Jeoltian seemed dismayed. His dog-like ears pointed downward, and his skin changed colors, making it look like it had sequins on it. Jeoltians were known for their emotionality and perceptiveness. Taking out a computerized notepad, the ambassador typed in some information.

"Very well," said the ambassador, "I'm Ambassador Neuralla. It is a pleasure to meet all of you."

Aida and the Itors seemed restless. They did not like the formalness of the occasion. Captain Bahm liked it even less as he had a perpetual look of concern.

"What will happen to our Star Jumper?" asked Bahm.

"It will stay here while you're on Jeolt," said Neuralla.

The ambassador put his hands out and showed the crew of the Star Jumper their way to a transport ship. They boarded the vessel and landed safely in Zi'Chu, the capital of Jeolt. Captain Bahm exited the transport and looked around the space and airport dock. Swarms of people passed before him. Atticus and the others followed him.

"Looks like we made it," said Bahm.

He put his arm around Atticus. Aida walked to them and stood beside them. As the Itors walked off the transport, some pedestrians showed interest and some fear at the sight of the fierce yet docile Itors.

"When will we make our way to King Kuckgo?" said Llub.

"Hold on, we need to get accustomed to our surroundings," said Bahm.

Atticus found a free ground transport to take them to the palace. He gathered everyone and told the driver they were ready. In a few seconds, they were flying among the sights and sounds of Zi'Chu.

When the ground transport touched down in front of the palace, Bahm tipped the driver. They met some statesmen who instructed them on where to find the court officials and King Kuckgo. The palace was awe-inspiring both inside and outside the complex.

King Kuckgo was found reclining in his garden. Atticus and Bahm both cleared their throats as they approached the king. They could tell he was in a good mood. His rainbow sequin-like skin moved gently across his body. King Kuckgo was wearing a virtual reality headset to play some games of pleasure. His ears pointed up when he noticed Bahm, Atticus, and the others approaching him. Atticus coughed again.

"Your royal highness, King Kuckgo, we are some sojourners in this galaxy, and we request safety on your planet and in your capital city," said Atticus confidently.

"Got straight to the point, eh?" Bahm murmured under his breath.

King Kuckgo took off his visor. Some attendants changed a plate of food for another, and another attendant gently fanned him. He grabbed a drink and then looked at the crew of the Star Jumper.

"There are plenty of sojourners in this galaxy. What makes you so special?" contended King Kuckgo.

"We all believe it would be in your best interests to grant safety for travelers on a Star Jumper," smirked Atticus.

"And who are you all exactly?" taunted King Kuckgo.

"This is Captain Bahm of the Star Union and Aida, a Humar who used to live on Fina. And a group of Itors led by Llub of Vinosa. They are the most honest and trustworthy Itors you will ever meet, sire. I am from one of the Independent Worlds called Stie Lux," affirmed Atticus.

King Kuckgo looked them over one after the other. His interest seemed to have perked up as the introduction went further. He licked his lips and plucked a fruit from the plate beside him. They all watched the king earnestly.

"All of you are far from home. As for what I expect…I just met someone from the Star Union and the Independent Worlds. To completely different political situations. I am guessing you have upset some renegade, or the Kernanites are after you," he surmised.

Aida grabbed Atticus' arm. She looked concerned. King Kuckgo looked at her closely. Her white skin shimmered in the light. Her green eyes looked firmly for a moment at Atticus.

"This isn't going as planned," stated Aida. "He is putting up too much resistance."

"So, what is your decision regarding your royal highness?" said Bahm.

"I have decided to grant you safe passage and harbor—if and only if you did not bring trouble with you. My military will perform a security sweep of your ship and a deep scan of the nebula. You're mine now," exclaimed the king.

Atticus lowered his head and tried to suppress feelings that somehow his freedom was being taken away. There was no sign of trouble, only the dead Star Union special operation soldiers on the civilian cruiser. The king sat up from his recliner.

"Many thanks, Your Royal Highness," said the Itors together in deep voices.

Atticus and the group were about to follow some court officials when what looked like berserks from the Eight Clans of Kiva came out of nowhere. Atticus and everyone froze in their steps. The personnel guarding the king opened fire on all five. Captain Bahm brought out his ion gun and ordered Aida to crouch behind a rock in the garden. Atticus followed his lead. One of the beserks struck an Itor. The Itors scattered and then brought out some weapons that Atticus never knew they had on them.

"I may be honest and trustworthy, but I am not a fool," said Llub as he fired some shots at the beserks.

An ion beam grazed the rock in front of Atticus and Captain Bahm. Atticus breathed heavily. He needed to collect himself and think about who could be attacking them. Captain Bahm held his position. He and Llub moved towards the beserks. Then, all of a sudden, some Jeoltian defense personnel fell wounded.

King Kuckgo was with them when they fell and quickly ran to the other side of the palace. It was too late. A berserk materialized next to him and shot him dead. The Itors roared in lament, and Aida let out a haunting scream. Then, the beserks disappeared. Smoke and embers of fire filled the garden.

Atticus was still behind the rock. The surprise attack had knocked him senseless. He woke up disoriented. He started to remember other similar situations from his childhood. Captain Bahm rushed over to King Kuckgo's side.

Blood dripped from the king's mouth. Bahm placed a medical badge on him to ease his pain and stabilize his body. King Kuckgo was starting to stutter something.

"I know…what they're after…immortality," said King Kuckgo.

"What about immortality?" exclaimed Bahm.

Llub rushed over to their side and roared again. The king was now dying. Attendants and relatives of the king spilled out of the palace. They were letting out screams of horror and lament.

Atticus was still behind the rock, but all he could think of was Aida and the cruiser's dead soldiers. By keeping quiet, he had risked Bahm's and Aida's lives.

Aida finally stood straight up, her legs shaking from the sudden attack. She looked over to Atticus, but his eyes were still closed. Mumbling to himself, wishing this had not happened. He wished he was back on Fina.

The king's relatives and court attendants moved closer to him. They grew more despondent as the king's life was ending. Some of them started to point and yell.

"Is that a Star Union soldier?" one said.

"He murdered the king! Death to the Star Union!" said another.

Aida went over to attend to one of the Itors, who had an ion beam hit. Captain Bahm read the readings on the medical badge. Llub got up and gathered the other Itors. They were trapped.

Atticus finally gathered his senses. He thought about this plan to return to his home. He pushed those thoughts away as he approached the king and took out his ion gun to protect Llub and Captain Bahm.

King Kuckgo was still mumbling, but then he stopped. The medical badge fell silent. Captain Bahm and Llub wandered over to Atticus and took him aside from the commotion.

"Do you think we should tell them that we saw the dead Star Union soldiers?" said Llub. "What do you think it meant seeing them in that civilian cruiser?"

"It was a warning, Llub. Someone wants the Star Union destroyed, and the Star Union itself was after something," said Atticus under hushed breath.

Captain Bahm did not back away while King Kuckgo was dying. *Was it true the Star Union could be after something?* Atticus thought. Bahm brushed aside the other Jeoltians. The crowd finally calmed down, and Bahm stepped back and let the Jeoltian doctors and medical attendants administer to King Kuckgo. He stepped away, facing towards everything that was happening.

He moved over to where Atticus and Llub were standing.

"What have you not been telling me?" demanded Bahm.

"Nothing. Nothing," said Atticus, defending himself.

Llub looked uncomfortable with Bahm asking these questions. He huffed every time he saw another Jeoltain give him an angry look. Aida covered her mouth in shock and went over to Bahm.

"I hate to sound obvious, but do you think someone is after us," said Aida.

"Yes, I do now. The king said they wanted something about immortality. The only thing that has anything to do with immortality where we are going is on Ergo. It's called the Chalice of Life," informed Bahm.

Atticus did not like where this was going from what it sounded like in the captain's mind. Everything was pointing at him during this tragedy, including the civilian cruiser. *Who is after what?* Atticus thought.

Captain Bahm had a perplexed look on his face, and then he looked at Atticus.

"Everyone these days wants something from everyone. The Kernanites want something big. And the other galaxy powers have fed off the conflict from the Kernanites' conquest," surmised Bahm.

Atticus tried to hack the palace's security system to see if there was any danger. Unfortunately, news of the attack on the king had spread into the capital. The group could hear yells demanding the Star Union soldier's blood and everyone else's. Atticus and Llub looked at each other. It seemed they could not keep their secret any longer.

IV

The funeral procession for King Kuckgo winded its way through the capital. The sojourners of the Star Jumper looked out from a balcony of a royal suite provided by Ambassador Neuralla, who was called in when the crowds started to accuse Captain Bahm, Atticus, and the others of murdering King Kuckgo. Despite their cordial relationship with the ambassador, the group no longer felt welcomed in Jeolt. Captain Bahm had remained quiet after the attack on King Kuckgo and barely spoke to Atticus. Today, Atticus decided to soothe his relationship with Captain Bahm.

"Do you have a minute?" said Atticus to Bahm.

Bahm looked like he was trying to brush off a frown on his face. He continued to look out over the balcony and crossed his arms over his chest. He let out a sigh.

"What haven't you been telling me, Atticus? It's certain now that the Kernanites and their allies are on our tail," stated Bahm.

Atticus attempted not to let his nervousness show through. Bahm looked at him intensely. Then, he looked away.

"It was the shipyard and the civilian cruiser we encountered, wasn't it?" questioned Bahm.

"Well…. I…. I," stammered Atticus.

Bahm grabbed Atticus' clothes on his chest. The captain stared him straight in the eye. Atticus returned the intimidating look in his eyes.

"We found some dead Star Union soldiers. They were special operations, and they were shot," said Atticus.

"What! Dead Star Union soldiers?" said Bahm.

"We didn't tell you because…. Because…," said Atticus.

Atticus could not think of a reason for their silence about the soldiers. Bahm loosened the grip on his clothes. A look of dismay swelled over Bahm's face.

"Why do you think the soldiers were dead?" said Atticus.

"It was a warning. Even though they were killed in the middle of the Utopian Nebula, we are supposedly safe. They must have gotten the attention of the Crinix or the Clans."

"The attack and death of King Kuckgo is a high-profile strike on the peace and order of the galaxy," stated Captain Bahm.

"What do we do next?" said Atticus.

"We need to leave Jeolt and the Utopian Nebula, Atticus. That's what," shot back Bahm.

"Will we get attacked? We are only halfway there to the Independent Worlds."

"This was the Itors destination," stated Bahm.

"What will we encounter once we leave the nebula?" said Atticus.

"Mond-Qu, a planet of ancient nations, is on the way," said Bahm, "It's a stopping point for fuel, food, and other necessities. They provide food for a large part of this side of the galaxy."

"The people of Mond-Qu are extremely religious," explained Atticus.

"We will need to stop there for a while to know if the Kernanites have spread out further in the galaxy if we do not encounter them on the way to Mond-Qu," said Bahm.

Atticus wondered about the Star Jumper. *Do we need a bit more heavily equipped ship? We need weapons,* he thought.

Atticus moved over to Aida. She looked lovely in some robes she got from the market. She looked like she was in deep thought.

"So, how are you feeling? Will you be stopping here, Aida?" pursued Atticus.

"Remember, my destination is the Independent Worlds. I was born into slavery. I have never experienced freedom. That's what the Independent Worlds will always represent to me despite all this talk of war."

"So that's a promise you will stay with us?" inquired Atticus.

"Yes. Plus, you guys look like you need a helping hand."

"The Itors will be staying here."

"I've heard Llub is separating from them. You know, Itors. He senses a challenge."

The commotion on the streets from the funeral procession seemed to have died down, and Atticus and the rest of the sojourners made their way into the royal suite. They would rest this morning and head to the space dock orbiting Jeolt. Atticus found a spot to lie down that he saw was comfortable. Aida decided to sleep beside him even though there was no more room.

When the group woke, the royal attendants saw their things taken aboard the Star Jumper. They transported everyone on the ground to the space dock. Captain Bahm bargained with the Jeoltians to provide the Star Jumper with a new guidance system and ion weapons.

The Star Jumper departed from the Jeoltian space dock. Atticus sat in the co-pilot's chair, and Bahm looked disgruntled that he had done so. Bahm's eyes remained fixed on the incredible colors of the nebula. After inputting the coordinates for leaving the nebula, they engaged the engines and entered hyperspace.

It took about a day to make it out of the Utopian Nebula. Once they did, the mood in the Star Jumper felt gloomy. The sudden attacks had demoralized them.

Atticus went over to Llub for some companionship. Llub had initially planned to stay with the Captain, Atticus, and Aida. Llub was looking through a virtuality visor when Atticus approached.

"So, are you glad you decided to go with us?" questioned Atticus to Llub.

Llub looked uneasy. He grunted, removed the visor, and placed it on a table before him. Llub, as an Itor, did not seem as threatened as the other did about the attack.

"Yes, I am glad to travel to the Independent Worlds. We know nothing about why the Kernanites are on the move or who will take their side next. They could be after me for all I know. I am no holy priest," warned Llub.

"Oh," said Atticus, "You are not convinced the Kernanites have ceased their moves of aggression in the galaxy."

"I can piece the situation together. The only people with whom I have anything in common are the dead Star Union soldiers we saw on the cruiser. I was once a Star Jumper pilot myself," informed Llub.

"Star Jumper pilot or none. You're one of us now. Someone just trying to make his way through the galaxy," opined Atticus.

Atticus heard Captain Bahm call through his communication badger. It was time for Atticus to take the pilot's chair. Atticus was not that eager. Aida looked at Atticus soothingly.

He had not sat in a pilot's chair in a while. The guidance system seemed to work, and the Star Jumper overall appeared to be in superb condition. He double-checked the system to see if any ships were in the vicinity.

"We'll reach Mond-Qu in a day," informed Bahm.

Atticus relaxed a bit and checked for incoming transmissions from Mond-Qu. There were none. For some reason, Aida was over by the science and operations console.

When they received transmissions from Mond-Qu, Atticus was elated. It was a peaceful transmission filled with Mond-Qu religiosity, and there was no sign of the Kernanites.

When the Star Jumper dropped out of hyperspace near Mond-Qu, he could see the colors of the clouds swirling in a marble-like fashion. It was a lush planet full of farmers and religious technocrats.

He docked the Star Jumper at a space dock orbiting the world. Instead of an ambassador meeting them, a monk met them. His long, cream-colored robes fell loosely over his body. He was a Uroc, a secretive race that little was known about in the galaxy. Slits on his throat were gills that Urocs used in their home world since they were semi-aquatic.

"Welcome to Mond-Qu! My name is Bescur. I am from the religious order called the Venit," he said solemnly.

He bowed to the Atticus group, and they all looked at each other, but then they reciprocated. Atticus did not want to make an enemy who violated a religion's code, so he let Captain Bahm take the lead.

"Hello, I'm Captain Reno Bahm of the Star Union," said Bahm.

"We've heard of you. We learned about the attack on King Kuckgo, and his life was taken."

Atticus immediately stood straight up and formal. He did not want Urocs not to let them on Mond-Qu. They were the gatekeepers and priests of this world. They had the title of Dol.

"Dol Bescur," said Atticus anxiously, "We appreciate the formalities and cordiality, but we need to get on the move."

"Very well. There is a village on the southernmost continent that could take you in. There is a monastery there. It is a nice place. It is chilly there right now, but it will warm up soon enough," said Dol Bescur.

"Thank you. Thank you very much," Atticus clasped his hands in appreciation and bowed.

The group of four boarded a shuttle bound for the village. Clouds rushed past them, and the closer they got to the ground, the more the gigantic flying serpents could be seen. They bent their necks and bodies in a corkscrew-like fashion and propelled themselves further.

The shuttle touched down on a landing pad. And, as soon as it powered down, the doors opened. Atticus ran out in ecstasy. Bahm looked at him quizzically.

"I thought I—mean—We—weren't going to make it," said Atticus.

Aida also looked thankful, unlike Llub, who was as prideful as ever. Dol Bescur had stayed with them to make sure their accommodations were met. They found the monastery, and there was room for four.

Atticus could hear the water trickle. There was a stream near the monastery. In the distance, they could listen to the hustle and bustle of a village. The people of Mond-Qu let most galaxy species worship their faith with them. Atticus and Aida decided to take a look around the monastery. It seemed that its occupants were mainly Urocs. Atticus took Aida to the stream. They both breathed sighs of relief.

Aida looked like she was enjoying her freedom. The two held each other's hand. In moments of freedom like these, she attracted Atticus. He wanted her to be free. Free as he was on and in every world he had encountered.

Atticus and Aida heard some loud splashes further downstream. To their astonishment, Llub was eating fish with his mouth. Aida giggled, and Atticus waved to see if Llub would recognize them. He did.

"Only in my home world have I seen so many delicious-looking delicacies," said Llub.

"Are you sure you can eat them?" questioned Atticus.

"I'm sure," said Llub.

Llub looked at the two holding hands. After noticing their affection, he was more attentive to what he was eating. The monastery sat back from the river on a hill. Atticus could hear chanting. He and Aida strode through the fields just outside the village and near the monastery. Mond-Qu was a peaceful world. Even the villagers were peaceful. The two went into the town, and Atticus bought Aida a wreath of flowers.

"Do you think we'll make it to Stie Lux and the other Independent Worlds," worried Aida.

"I'm sure. I'll ask for a blessing from one of the monks so that our journey is safe."

Aida and Atticus collected themselves. They heard noises approaching them. Atticus stood in the middle of the street, and Aida stepped back from the intrusion. Atticus peered into the distance, and then his eyes focused. It was some ruffian from the village. He thought Mond-Qu lived in harmony, but he seemed from off-world. Atticus then knew the male was a Pirna. They were charlatans like Itors but had a good side. This Pirna was deeply disturbing the villagers.

He saw Atticus. He then shouted something in a language Atticus could not understand. He pointed at Aida.

"I want that lovely woman," he said.

"Well, you cannot have her," defended Atticus.

The Pirna was about Atticus's build, so he was not intimidated. The Pirna shoved Atticus, but Atticus did not push back at the Pirna. He did not want to get exiled from Mond-Qu.

"How much will it take for me to have her? My name is Yort," inquired the Pirna while he took some air.

"You cannot have her," firmly stated Atticus.

"She's just a Humar. Beautiful, but a Humar nonetheless," said Yort.

Yort lunged at Aida and missed grabbing her arms. Aida screamed, and she took to Atticus' side. She then backed away from the fight.

"I am not for sale," she said.

"A Pirna saying says, " 'Your eyes will tell you what is good to buy. And, they never lie'," he cajoled.

He took out what seemed like a ritual knife he could have gotten from the criminal underworld and swiped at Atticus and Aida. He took another try, and this time, Atticus blocked his arm. Striking his metal wristband, Atticus brought his arm to the ground.

Yort shouted something. More Pirna appeared from the crowd. They seemed like wanting a fight. Atticus pushed Aida out of the way, and he grabbed Yort's knife.

The other Pirna lunged at Atticus, but he blocked every single one of them. Atticus gesticulated at them to move on, flaring his arms up and down so they could see they had lost. The Pirna left. Yort assessed Atticus again.

"You're not from around here," touted Yort.

"No, I'm not," smirked Atticus.

"I'll give you one more time before I strike you," said Yort.

"Go ahead," beckoned Atticus.

Yort took a whip-like weapon out and wielded it in the air. Atticus fought and grabbed a long piece of wood from a villager's cart. Yort's weapon suddenly flew at Atticus, and Atticus stuck out the piece of wood. The whip wrapped around the piece of wood, but Atticus gained the upper hand instead of Yort. Yort fell face-first onto the ground, and he let out a moan.

He was beaten. Atticus grabbed Aida, and they left the village. The twin moons of Mond-Qu showed brightly in the night sky. Aida and Atticus were on the porch holding each other. It had been a while since Atticus had touched the feminine. He had been caught in the thrill of being so far from home and free. He did not want anything to ruin this moment. The trickle of the stream brought solace to him.

Suddenly, someone opened the door to the porch. It was Bahm. He held some ale in his hand. He looked away from Aida and Atticus. He seemed to disapprove of their fondness for each other.

Llub was heard snoring in one of the rooms in the monastery. Bahm walked out to the stream. And Atticus and Aida separated. They knew they must reach the Independent Worlds first and foremost. Their lives depended on it, but Atticus knew love had no limits. He looked up at the night sky. Filaments of star clusters twinkled in the night sky. Bahm walked back onto the porch and briefly stopped in front of the two. Atticus had never seen Bahm like this. Atticus looked for a nod of approval, but there was none.

The night went on, and Atticus and Aida continued to look up at the stars. Whatever was out there could not stop them now. Or, at least, they thought.

V

Atticus and Aida woke up in the same room. In the attached wing of the monastery, they smelled breakfast cooking in a large kitchen. They moved into the day room to eat. Llub was cooking breakfast, but Bahm was still asleep. Aida eyed the delicious meal Llub was cooking. Then, she turned her attention toward Atticus.

"So, I have been meaning to ask: What did King Kuckgo say before he died," said Aida.

"Oh, nothing, some old wise tell about the Chalice of Life—a supposedly magical object. It is beyond the science of our current understanding."

"Oh? Nothing is really beyond us in this galaxy. I am a Humar from Fina and understand most things."

"That is not what I meant. Some things are currently beyond our galactic understanding. Further, it has a religion safeguarding it," stated Atticus.

"Which religion?" Aida looked around and smiled. Captain Bahm came downstairs and sat at the other end of the table.

"Well, the people of Mond-Qu adhere to the Cidnor religion and supposedly protected the Chalice of Life centuries ago."

"Have you ever been to a monastery like this?" questioned Aida.

"Never. We should take a look around more, though," said Atticus.

Llub wanted to start a conversation with Bahm. Aida and Atticus continued to converse. Llub then began directing his conversation further at Bahm.

"Captain, did you expect me to make it this far on this journey and stay with you despite our challenges?" said Llub.

"I am a man of my word, so I took your word," murmured Bahm.

He was hunched over something that looked like soup. He brought out a star map. Atticus spotted what he was doing.

"That is my star map, you know, Bahm," stated Atticus.

"Well, I was just borrowing it. To finish mapping our journey to the Independent Worlds," informed Bahm.

"Where do you think this Chalice of Life is?" inquired Aida to Bahm.

Bham looked puzzled at Aida's question.

"Well, for all we know, it's somewhere on Mond-Qu. The adherents to the religion here are sworn to protect it. I've never bothered to come to Mond-Qu or research the story. I am not that kind of person. I am more empirical, you know," said Bahm.

Atticus finished eating. He was growing restless already, and he knew his mind and body demanded some exploration. Atticus stood up with Aida and decided to tour the monastery independently.

"You two children have fun!" quipped the Captain.

Atticus gesticulated an insult, and Aida giggled.

The door to the front of the monastery creaked open as Aida and Atticus entered the old building. Atticus grabbed a light stick, which was dark inside. They both looked around them.

"They sure don't like lights in here," said Aida in a shaky voice. "Maybe we shouldn't go any further. It's not our place."

"What do you mean?" said Atticus, "We haven't even set foot in it."

Atticus encouraged Aida to go further, and she agreed. The monastery had five levels built around a central complex with dark halls, and it was filled with silence.

"Where are all the monks?" wondered Aida.

"They are out in the fields or at their workstations. I want to go to the central complex and see what we can find," directed Atticus.

They were at the third level when they heard a rushing sound. It was not wind. Then, particles of light filled the hallway.

"I think we found what everyone has been looking for."

They followed the light up another level. By the time they reached the fourth level, they had entered the central complex. The center of the complex looked like a shrine, with several rooms inside and glistening walls. Atticus and Aida went further into the shrine, and Atticus held a light stick in the dark.

In the center of one of the rooms in the shrine, there looked like a place for an object to stand. Atticus pressed the light stick to fill the room with more light. When he did, the pedestal opened, and the Chalice of Life stood. Atticus and Aida's eyes grew wide with wonder. This chalice had been heard in legends for thousands of generations. It was said that if taken into battle, it could give the possessor's army immortality, new life, or more.

This must have been why we saw the dead Star Union soldiers and the attack on King Kuckgo. Why was it at this monastery, though? thought Atticus. This monastery had no fame to speak of in the galaxy except that it resided on Mond-Qu, and the religion of Cidnor had protected the Chalice of Life for centuries.

Atticus went through his utility belt and pockets and found a transporter device. It would transport the device onto one of the shuttles to the space dock above Mond-Qu. Atticus aligned the devices, but a Uroc monk entered the room before he could.

"What are you doing," said the monk.

"I'm......... doing research," stuttered Atticus.

The monk looked both shocked and dismayed. A few seconds after the monk appeared, an alarm sounded. Atticus transported the Chalice, but the monk blocked the door when he and Aida turned around to leave.

"That Chalice has remained hidden for centuries," he informed, "And, during these times of rumors of war, someone bigger than you may want to take it. I have taken an oath of non-violence so that you may go, but not far."

"Uh…very well…thank you," exclaimed Atticus as the alarm continued to sound. Aida covered her ears and hurried along with Atticus. Both of them made it to the room where breakfast had been served. Bahm looked at them with vexed concern and anger. Llub huffed and banged the table.

"I knew it!" he said. "You cannot trust a Stie Luxian with a Humar if your life depended on it."

When Atticus looked at Bahm, Bahm looked smug. Bahm pointed outside and then up to the sky. Atticus went outside and found Star Union destroyers in the sky. The metallic, seamless hulls of the destroyers shined in the day sun.

"So, you brought with you the Star Union. I knew you were hiding something—exactly what—I never knew," he confessed.

He looked over at Llub, who was outside looking up at the Star Union destroyers. They heard fighting and the sound of ion guns being fired in the village. Screams from the villagers were heard. The Itor became unsettled and roared in opposition. Atticus walked over to him.

"What do we do next, Llub?" said Atticus, "You are more of a fighter than I."

"We cannot let them know we are here. I suggest we go into the wilderness outside the monastery and village," he ordered.

Atticus ran back inside and grabbed Aida. Llub quickly followed them. None of them acknowledged Bahm. Star Union Soldiers were catching up to them as they exited the monastery grounds, but they stopped at the monastery. Atticus, Aida, and Llub waded through a river and ran through some farmland. They finally reached the wild hills outside the village and monastery.

They went through the underbrush and forests of the hills until they eventually found some old caves. The caves were on the side of a mountain, looking over the river delta of farmland. They could see smoke rising from the village.

"I think we are relatively safe," said Atticus. Aida looked intently at the scene developing on the flat lands of the river and farmlands. She did not utter a word.

"Captain Bahm revealed our location to the Star Union," said Llub, "I just know it."

Atticus did not want to think about it. Bahm's shunning ultimately erodes the trust between him, Atticus, and the rest of the group. Atticus looked up at the Star Union destroyers. Some were moving in the other direction in a low orbit. *Why would they attack?* he thought. The Kernanites must be closer than any of them thought. Llub went further into the cave and made camp.

"We won't eat warm food tonight so that a fire won't give our location," said Llub.

"Do you think they are after someone or someone like we thought at the civilian cruiser," wondered Atticus.

"It's hard to say. The Kernanites must be conquering worlds faster than us Itors have thought to push out the Star Union into the territory of Mond-Qu."

"I don't believe what I am seeing," said Aida with a quiver in her voice, and she grew noticeably more distraught; she looked over at Atticus, who gave her a comforting look. Somehow, Atticus knew that Bahm had revealed their location or that the Star Union had gotten it elsewhere. Atticus was not a telepath, but he knew Bahm did not like getting found out by only some simpletons in his eyes and fellow travelers. The group decided to go into some higher caves and make camp. Smoke stopped coming from the village, but the Star Union destroyers were still in orbit around Mond-Qu.

Aida sat around the fire. A calm wind blew through the wild hills. Atticus sat over with Aida, bringing his arm over her shoulders. She, who was once enslaved, was desperate for freedom, and rightfully so. Other worlds thought of Aida's species and place in society differently. Aida had not seen many other worlds then besides Fina, as she was taken into slavery as a child. She seemed to be taking the scenery in breath by breath.

The group of three sat by the fire until late at night. Before bed, Atticus thought of Aida. She did not seem upset at Bahm's sudden betrayal. Atticus decided to ask Aida about him.

"What motivated Bahm to alert the Star Union?" asked Atticus.

"I don't think you will like the answer," quipped Aida. "I may not have practiced all my Humarian abilities, but I know for one, he was motivated by two ideal values: honor and duty. You would think he would have forgotten those, but something triggered them inside the man."

"But why? Why would he choose based on those values he only acted on long ago?"

"Fighting and war changes people. Everyone knows that. It was what he was accustomed to."

Atticus rested beside Aida. He wished he had known her before all this happened before he had to go outside the known and Independent Worlds for safety. Llub sat on the other side of the fire. He started to drift off to sleep. And, before he knew it, his eyes closed.

When the morning came, beams of sunlight filled the cave. Llub was awake, looking at the plains and marshes below the hills. He seemed content, and then he grimaced at Llub.

"You found something, didn't you in the monastery," inquired Llub.

Atticus smiled back at him. *Were Itors telepaths, too?* Atticus mused over what could happen next. They needed to pass the Star Union destroyers and reach the space dock to get the Star Jumper. The Star Union destroyers were still in low orbit.

Atticus felt a presence. For a moment, everything around him became surreal. Atticus let out a cry of surprise. Adia laughed behind him. Her green eyes turned into a lighter, brighter green, and her white, crystal-like skin shined in the morning sunlight. She looked unlike anything Atticus had seen from the worlds he had been to or his home world, Stie Lux. Aida placed her hand on his shoulder, and images of his home flashed before him. His deepest fears and the heights of his happiness were realized and explored.

Aida delved deeper into Atticus's mind. Then, the telepathic link between Aida and Atticus overpowered both, pushing them to the ground, and both screamed. Aida rolled over on her side and then stood, holding her hand to her head.

Atticus awoke with his head on the ground. He squinted his eyes and moved around a little, and as soon as he did, a pain went up through his back and shoulders. He started to stutter some words.

"Wha….t…hap… penned?" he said to Aida and Llub.

Llub smiled and roared and then thumped his chest. He took a step back as Aida approached. She was holding some bandages and other medicine. Llub looked annoyed.

"Couldn't you use some of your special powers, Humar, to heal your fling?" adamantly questioned Llub.

Aida did not like what she heard, so she bared her teeth. She rolled over Atticus as he coughed. Her eyes scanned his entire body and darted everywhere.

"This…this…has never happened before, Atticus and Llub," said Aida in an anxious voice, "Did you see anything before you blacked out and hit the ground?"

"I saw flashes of images but nothing more. I felt a presence or something," said Atticus. Aida looked at his head for cuts and bruises. She closed her eyes.

She opened her eyes and said, "The Kernanites must be onto our trail. The telepathic link started to break from stress. It was being used by someone else. The Kernanites can gather our locations and strategies through mind view or put—by getting inside our minds."

"A Kernanite would never attempt to get inside the mind of an Itor. It would be two confusing, too primitive yet advanced," exclaimed Llub. Itors were known for their resistance to telepathy and its effects. Aida continued to attend to Atticus's wounds. Atticus started to get up and push her away from helping him more when he knew he was fine.

He grabbed Aida's hand and locked eyes. "I'm fine. Don't worry. We need to get on moving," ordered Atticus.

"Did you want me to say on Mond-Qu?" said Llub.

"I'm not sure. We are about halfway there to the Independent Worlds. I'm trying to avoid what I think is next, or maybe we can go around it. We need to get up to the space dock where the Star Jumper is," said Atticus.

"What's next exactly?" said Llub.

"Unfortunately, it's a Star Union planet on the fringes of their space. It's called Ergh, and it's mostly desert. We can use it to block the Kernanites so they will not bother. They would never start an open conflict with the Star Union," surmised Atticus as he looked out over the plains and farmlands of Mond-Qu.

"We also need to check in on what brought the encounters with the Kernanites—if it has been remotely detected," said Aida.

"You're referring to the attack on King Kuckgo, what we found in the monastery, and now this aggressive strike by them?" said Atticus.

The twin suns of Mond-Qu rose gently from the horizon and cast light on the hills, making them green and red. The group gathered their things and patched in communications to the space dock orbiting Mond-Qu. The Star Jumper was ready for them. It was only a matter of time before Kernanite striking attempts would come to Atticus, Aida, and Llub.

VI

Atticus gained a shuttle from a group of farmers to take them to the space dock. By the time they made it up to the space dock, it was the end of the Mond-Qu day. There were guards stationed at every junction on the space dock as the space dock was on high alert because of the orbiting star destroyers. Atticus managed to bargain with one of the security personnel to gain access to the Star Jumper.

The space dock ship bay doors opened, and the Star Jumper made its way out and made a hyperspace jump to Ergh, the Star Union planet that would provide cover from the Kernanites. Before departing the Mond-Qu space dock, Atticus outfitted the Star Jumper with Star Union emblems and spaceship designs.

When the Star Jumper dropped out of hyperspace, Atticus and the others were surprised that it was seen as part of the Star Union's fleet. Atticus found a space dock, outfitting the Star Jumper with the Star Union logo and designs to camouflage the Star Jumper well. Atticus, Llub, and Aida exited the Star Jumper and went to a transport.

While traveling, Atticus ensured they had camouflaged themselves well with Star Union uniforms. They found a transport ready to depart to Ergh. Atticus spoke one of the Star Union's languages, and the group was let on board.

The transport flew through the harsh Ergh atmosphere and violent dust storms as it approached the surface. The people of Ergh lived at and below the planet's surface. The indigenous people of Ergh looked more like some form of primate Atticus once saw as a child in a jungle world named Y'Car.

They eventually found their way to one of the major cities—Setya. Llub was getting tired of all the traveling and demanded some drinks. Atticus and Aida were hesitant, but they eventually agreed.

All three of them took a seat at a local bar. Llub was already busy chitchatting with a local. Atticus decides to drink for himself, but Aida decides to pass.

"So, what do you know, my friend, about this aggression by the Kernanites?" questioned Llub to an Erghian.

"I don't think it's aggression. I think it's more like paranoia by them. The galaxy has changed so much in the last seventy-five years that they feel left out," said the local.

Atticus attempted to tune their conversation out and focus on Aida. He had not been in a bar since Fina when he found Aida. Atticus liked traveling; it reminded him of his childhood. Aida appeared not as gloomy as on the trip or the other planets.

A computer pad filled with news from throughout the galaxy was at the bar. Atticus picked it up and began to read. Although its pages astonished him. In them was a biographical profile of Captain Bahm.

Atticus's eyes read the article in the newspaper line by line. For a moment, he forgot Llub and Aida were sitting with him. He kept on reading the article.

The article said Captain Reno Bahm of the Fourth Fleet was wanted for treason. It did not say why he was wanted for treason, only that he was once a captain of the Fourth Fleet. The music in the bar was getting loud, and the patrons were a bit noisy. Llub appeared intoxicated, and so did Aida.

Adia touched Atticus's chest and then his lips. Aida's upfront behavior took Atticus aback. She spun in a circle and went for Llub. The Itor laughed in delight.

Then, she spun around and stuck out her hand. Her white crystal skin looked flushed around her cheeks, but it looked like she was having fun. She came closer.

"Wanna dance?" she asked Atticus.

Atticus started to get a lump in his throat at the suggestion. Aida is fulfilling a dream. She was not nervous after having so many drinks.

Atticus took Aida's hand, and they went to the band playing in front of the bar. Atticus whispered into an assistant's ear the song he wanted to play. The band stopped and then molded their music into different beats.

As Aida and Atticus danced, others joined. Atticus had not spent much time noticing them, only not to bump into them while he was dancing. As the song ended, he saw a figure on the other side of the dance floor. The figure was wearing a hooded cloak. Atticus took note of the figure because it was peculiar to him.

When the song ended, there was applause throughout the bar, and requests for another were shouted. Atticus put his arm around Aida. He liked where this was going. But what about Captain Bahm? He was already in trouble; why *did he take the side of the Star Union?* Atticus was contemplating all of this while he waited for the band. Then, he heard Adia scream. He felt her slip from his arm, and she fell away. He sharply turned around and saw the hooded figure take Aida.

Atticus had his gun, so he opened fire on the cloaked figure. The shots bounced right off the figure, and Aida had enough strength to rip his hood off. What was under the hood shocked Atticus. It was a Kernanite. Blue ether came from his eyes, and its black skin blended with the darkened bar. The Kernanite let out a grizzly sound. Atticus did not know if it was in his language or not. Atticus tried to stun the Kernanite, but the shots were always deflected. Llub came barreling at him from the bar, and the Kernanite used a teleportation device to take him to the other side of the bar. Llub hit a table, smashed it, and ended up on the ground.

Atticus could feel the opportunities to have Aida back slip away from him. The Kernanite went out the front door and into the hustle and bustle of Setya. Llub got up on the bar floor and ran after the Kernanite.

Startled screams were everywhere in the bar. Atticus and Llub went out into the Erghian night and sandblasted them. He could only guess what the Kernanite wanted with Aida. Atticus went back into the bar to gather his things.

Llub stayed outside as he gathered his things. He was putting away one of his computer pads when he noticed it said another computer pad was tracking something. He looked at it more closely, and the computer pad recorded sound and video. He turned on the link to show Aida the computer pad. Atticus could only hear the Kernanite and Aida's muffled cries.

How could he get to her? he thought. Llub looked dismayed and a bit sad about Aida's kidnapping. He told Llub that Aida had been successfully tracked, and Llub suddenly had a look of hope on his face.

Atticus did not want to sleep at night and did not think he could. Atticus and Llub found a ground transport and began following the computer pad tracker's route. It took them throughout Setya and its borders, but they had no luck finding Aida.

They must find Aida soon. They decided to get some sleeping accommodations. Looking up in the early morning sky, he saw Star Union destroyers had dropped out of hyperspace. It was their world, thought Atticus, even though it was on the fringe of their space. Soon, space and planet transports were seen coming from the Star Union destroyers. The Star Union military was weary of species not fully part of the Union, and anyone who did not look indigenous to a planet was generally shunned.

Atticus and Llub went inside their accommodations. He looked in the mirror. His jawline would make him stick out on Ergh. Once morning came, he wrapped his face in cloth. The smoothness of his brow was the only part that gave him away as an off-worlder. Llub was obvious, but Atticus still wrapped his face in cloth to make it less noticeable.

When Atticus and Llub awoke from a short sleep, they heard a commotion coming from outside where they were sleeping. When Atticus stepped outside, it looked like there was a sandstorm. Atticus looked closely, and space-to-ground transports touched down only about half a mile from the borders of the city of Setya. Atticus and Llub grabbed their things and searched for Aida.

When they were outside, they crouched and ran to the other side of the street to avoid being seen by the Star Union. It was only when they neared their transport that they knew the intent of the Star Union. Shots were fired at them. Atticus and Llub ducked behind a container. Soldiers from the Star Union emptied from the transports. Even though the Star Union soldiers were wearing helmets, Atticus could hear them say something that he recognized. He recognized the names Stie Lux and Llub. They were talking about them.

Atticus' breathing became quicker as the soldiers scoured the area. Llub remained calm but soon directed Atticus to a room that meandered away from the main areas of Setya. Atticus readied his gun, but Llub made motions not to engage the soldiers yet.

Llub took out a scanner and pointed it toward the Star Union soldiers. They wore upgraded army uniforms, which their ion guns could not penetrate. Llub and Atticus made it to the top of a roof. They both looked down as the Star Union soldiers filled the city. People quickly got out of their way, and some screamed. The Star Union had a galaxy-wide famous military, but it liked to remain separated and keep it at a distance.

Atticus was sweating, so he pushed himself to the ground just enough to let him see what was happening below him. Llub continued to scan the area. Then, he sat the scanner down.

"I have an idea, Atticus. If we cannot penetrate their armor, we must find something that will," explained Llub.

"Look at all of those containers. I scanned them, and they carry a liquid that explodes when exposed to an ion blast. We could overheat one of our ion guns. It injures some soldiers, creates a distraction, and by us some time."

Atticus looked at him like he was crazy. He remembered Itors had good intuition and senses, so he trusted him more but still thought he was crazy. He gave him a hint not to start his plan. In a moment, Llub pushed up and down on his ion gun and tied it to a rope to carry it down to the containers. The ion gun would be dropped from up above the containers. More than several soldiers were passing by, and it looked like it would be a good hit and a distraction.

Llub let the ion gun from a rope. Once the guns hit the containers, the program initiated an overload, and then a bright light was seen, followed by several explosions. Screams of surprise were heard by the Star Union soldiers. Llub stood up, roared in triumph, and puffed out his chest. The blast cleared the way for Llub and Atticus to make it through and down the streets of Setya.

Thoughts raced through Atticus' mind. Of all the species he knew of in the galaxy, he never thought he would pair up with an Itor and take out Star Union soldiers. Llub and Atticus continued to run until they reached ground-to-space dock transport.

The glow from Setya gently faded into the distance. As they approached the space dock from the opposite direction, Atticus collected himself. He thought about their cargo on board, the Chalice of Life. There was no question that the Star Union knew who they were, but maybe they did not realize that Kernanites were also after him. It would be nice to have an extra hand. He thought about Captain Bahm. Captain Bahm had turned their backs on the group.

Atticus calmed himself down. If Captain Bahm was wanted for treason by the Star Union, he could not stay in their territory. He linked the computer pad tracker to the Star Jumper. It showed Aida's life signs on board a ship in hyperspace heading toward Kernanite territory. Llub sounded exhausted. He asked the on-board kitchen robot for some food.

Atticus piloted the Star Jumper in the direction of Kernanite Territory. Llub got in the co-pilot's chair. And Atticus engaged the engine.

Llub and Atticus also ensured the Star Union was not pursuing them. Atticus knew what he was doing. He was taking one of the revered and mysterious relics, the Chalice of Life, into the hands of the enemy. His plan would work, and he knew why. Atticus was talking to Llub when he suddenly felt a presence.

Images filled his head. There were black figures everywhere, and the glow of a moon was seen. Suddenly, he heard muffled words. Someone was saying, "Help me!" Atticus grabbed the computer pad tracker. It had Aida's signal, then lost it. He programmed the Star Jumper computer to intensify the tracker's scanning capability. It firmly picked up Aida's life signs in Kernanite space on the planet of Xo'Ti.

Atticus looked over at Llub.

"Llub, I think Aida is trying to contact me using some Humar telepathic ability," explained Atticus.

Llub looked down at the tracker. His brow furrowed. He let out a big puff of air.

"Aida's is a Humar. I would say she is in danger, but she seems to be taking care of herself," said Llub.

Llub was irritated. They were going in the opposite direction of the Independent Worlds now. Atticus knew what awaited him back at home. His reputation as a no-good maverick would be forgotten if he brought back the Chalice of Life and surveyed the Kernanites.

He must save Aida first. The presence in his head was getting more and more intense. He tried to calm himself down, knowing Aida was attempting to communicate with him. Suddenly, Atticus could see Aida.

She was in a building with many windows. She was held down to the floor. Some prison chains were on Aida. Moonlight was streaming through the room she was put in.

In the background, the blue ethereal eyes of Kernanites could be seen. Atticus felt like Aida's presence was getting strong enough to make him talk to her, but so were the Kernanites. Atticus finally telepathically said, "I'm on my way," to Aida, but as soon as he did, the eyes of a Kernanite blocked his telepathic sight.

VII

Llub was piloting while Atticus slept on the way to the planet of Xo'Ti inside Kernanite Territory. Suddenly, Atticus woke up and looked around the Star Jumper. It was like she was there again, lying beside Atticus. The presence of Aida did not leave Atticus this time. What he felt was strength and resiliency. Even though the Kernanites had taken Aida, she was fighting back with all her power.

Kernanites were an ancient race to Atticus and, more so, Llub. Llub was from a younger race than Atticus. Kernanites inhabited a galaxy region called the Doldrums by Atticus's race. It was known for tumultuous space flight, and Kernanites received little outside contact from the rest of the galaxy. Eventually, Kernanites grew jealous of what lay outside their realm and only wanted to conquer and destroy. Kernanites were known for their immense powers. They could travel into other dimensions, were telepaths, and their life spans were long—about 500 years.

In case a Kernanite might contact them telepathically, Atticus told Llub to look for any odd behavior. Itors were viewed as ignorant in the galaxy, but Atticus wished he could resist the powers of a telepath this time. Unfortunately, he enjoyed experiencing the powers of a telepath like Aida, but not the Kernanites.

Atticus went to the center of the Star Jumper and pulled up a star map. Xo'Ti was about 50 clicks away. Xo'Ti was an ice world. Atticus had heard stories of Xo'Ti. It was a center of worship for the Kernanites. Atticus was studying the landing sites of Xo'Ti when suddenly, a black figure with blue vapor from its eye sockets invaded his mind. He dropped the computer pad.

"Llub, it's a Kernanite. He's inside my mind. Think quick. Do something," exclaimed Atticus to Llub.

Llub left the Star Jumper pilot seat and switched to artificial intelligence piloting. He then ran over to Atticus, placed his hand on his forehead, and prayed.

"The Kernanites are using their magic. Itors are immune to it," said Llub.

Atticus' race—the Stie Luxians—was not religious. They were clever farmers who were technologically savvy with a good fighting instinct. Atticus was shaken up about the intrusive Kernanites. What was he—or she—trying to do? Even though the Kernanites might know where they are and if they are heading in their direction, they must continue.

Llub went back to piloting the Star Jumper. Atticus studied the map of Xo' Ti and read ancient texts about the Kernanites. The Star Jumper dropped out of hyperspace outside the twin moons of Xo'Ti.

"I'm scanning the area around Xo'Ti," said Llub.

"Understood," said Atticus.

"Atticus, come look at this."

Llub pulled up a schematic that the scan created. It terrified Llub and Atticus. Two or three fleets of ships dotted with space stations in between filled the screen.

"They don't look like they know we are here," said Llub.

Atticus ran scan after scan for Aida. He swept both moons and hacked the computer systems of the Kernanite fleets to scan the surface of Xo'Ti. He was finally successful in finding Aida. She was in Kalendiraz—the central city of worship on the planet of Xo'Ti. Many outsiders did not know who or what the Kernanites worshipped. As the Star Jumper went to the dark side of Xo'Ti, the planet twinkled with the lights of the cities below.

Llub got up from the pilot's chair and accessed the main frame of the computer on the Star Jumper. Atticus finished plotting how they would approach the hostage situation. The Star Jumper jolted as Llub diverted energy to another system.

"We're going to teleport down to the surface," said Llub. "I'll give our teleportation signatures a cloak so we will not be detected, and if they try, the encryption code will give us time."

"Let's get to it then," said Atticus.

They both went to the back of the Star Jumper to stand on sensors. Llub pressed some Star Jumper consoles, and they were teleported. In a moment, they were on the surface and in Kalendiraz in a massive complex. They both brought out their ion guns and crouched along the wall. The Kernanites widely used artificial intelligence. Some advanced robots took the form of different species. Atticus and Llub used camouflage technology to hide their visible presence.

The closer they got to where Aida's signature was coming from, the more robots with weapons came at them. The enclosure was massive. Using encryptions, they decoded and opened the giant doors of the room. The camouflage technology worked because, as soon as they opened the door, a group of Kernanites were on the other side. Blue ether pulsated from their eyes, and their black, leathery-like skin emitted a smell. The Kernanites stood tall with armor covering themselves. Their language, at times, sounded horrendous to Llub and Atticus. They covered their ears and put translators inside their ears.

For a moment, Atticus could understand a word or two. He listened more closely. As they continued going through the front of the room, he picked up on some Kernanites saying what sounded like Aida's name.

When Atticus and Llub made it past the room, they saw a platform with a figure lying down. It was Aida. They both halted. This was too easy. They approached the platform, but then their camouflage technology started to glitch.

One of the Kernanites shouted something to a group on the other side. They had seen them. Atticus and Llub put shields on their suits and armor. Atticus felt his stomach almost curl up into a ball. They were so close to rescuing Aida.

Then suddenly, Aida stood up on the platform. A light beam went up through Aida, and vibrations shook the room. The vibrations were powerful enough to shake Atticus and Llub to the floor and the Kernanites.

The light beam dissolved into the room's darkness as soon as it appeared. Atticus and Llub ran over to Aida. She was curled up, clutching her legs, shivering, and naked.

When Atticus wanted to teleport back to the Star Jumper, Llub was hit by an ion weapon from the Kernanites. They ran to shield themselves on the other side of the platform. Llub clutched his shoulder.

"I've been hit," he said.

"Try to strengthen the teleportation signature so we can get out of here," yelled Atticus.

Atticus looked around the room to see what could cause a loss in their teleportation signal. It looked like a hidden temple with statues, columns, and a dome.

While they were crotched on the other side of the room, shielded by a protrusion of a platform, several Kernanites teleported to their side. They hit Atticus and Llub with stunning weapons, and both Atticus and Llub fell to the ground instantly. Atticus was pushed onto the wall of the temple. And so was Llub. A Kernanite came forth from the group of Kernanites, striking them.

His skin was black, but this time with red stripes. The blue of the Kernanite's eyes flickered in the dim lightning. He was more significant than the rest and had a generally good build. He looked like he was analyzing Llub and Atticus.

"So, you brought the Humar to me," grinned the Kernanite.

"We did not bring you anyone," yelled Atticus to the Kernanite.

"Do you not know the price of a Humar in my religion," he said. "They are priceless. And, what makes the situation better is you came after the Humar even with all the warnings."

The Kernanite brought out a knife. It looked ritualistic to Atticus. He held it to Aida's arm.

"Do you not know what she could do for my people?" said Atticus.

"We live forever with the blood of Humars. Humars are good, either dead or alive, to us. This one seems even more special than the others we have recently caught. Atticus searched his mind. All he could think about was how he wanted to return home. He did not know much about Aida's species; the galaxy has many species. *Why her?* he thought.

"My name is Ba'Gam," said the Kernanite. "You have come to the right region of the galaxy if you want to live forever."

"I have no intention," said Atticus.

"And where are you from, young man?" questioned Ba'Gam.

"I'm from Stie Lux, an Independent World," he stammered back

"You are far from home," stated Ba'Gam.

Llub snorted and got perturbed at the Kernanite. Llub reached for an ion grenade. Ba'Gam saw the move by Llub and shot an ion shackle at Llub, jamming his arm into the wall.

"You won't go far," said Ba'Gam.

Ba'Gam commanded the other Kernanites around him. They picked up Aida and then shackled Atticus to the wall. Atticus and Llub continue to struggle to set themselves free.

Aida was thrown back into the middle of the room on the platform. Sensors started to scan her, and the Kernanites everywhere in the room jeered. Ba'Gam remained quiet.

Atticus was shouting Aida's name. He felt like he was going to lose her at any moment. Suddenly, Aida's presence entered his mind. She was calm but unconscious.

"Do not be afraid, Atticus," she said, "I'm sorry for not telling you everything about me. It's been like this for centuries with the Kernanites."

"What do you mean? None of that is true, Aida. I have seen it with my own eyes—the freedom you have had. We can change things. For the better," struggled Attiucs.

Aida seemed conscious again, but she was still in Atticus' thoughts. Suddenly, she began floating above the platform. And, then, the shackles of Llub and Atticus were destroyed by some power. Atticus and Llub both looked at each other. It was Aida. Some of the Kernanites looked like they were about to shoot Aida. Before they could, orbs shot out of Aida's body. The orbs stunned them to the floor.

Ba'Gam ran to another doorway leading further into the complex. Aida's body hoovered and shined until the Kernanites ran from the room. Llub got up from the floor and ran over to Aida.

"No, don't," shouted Atticus. "She's going through something. Don't you feel it?"

"I feel like we should get out of here," said Llub.

Atticus looked over Aida's body. Her presence did not diminish while slipping in and out of consciousness. Aida was telling the story of her race. She was telling him why she was there.

Her species was not just a slave race on her home planet. It was a profoundly spiritual one, and its spiritual abilities were coveted. When the Humar met the Kernanites, the Kernanites were a slowly dying race again. After experimenting with captive Humars, the Kernanites learned they could increase their lifespans and senses and obtain latent abilities like telepathy.

As for Aida, she was different. Somehow, she was more powerful than an ordinary Humar. She could communicate with the gods of the Kernanites on various astral planes. Eventually, Aida came back to consciousness. She looked into the eyes of Atticus. She looked like she did not want it stopped.

In Atticus's thoughts, she communicated that this was not how it was supposed to be. Her mission was to offer herself up to the gods of the Kernanites. She started to push Atticus away from her.

"No, no, no, this isn't how it is supposed to be," said Aida.

Llub looked down at Aida and Atticus. He had strengthened the teleportation signature, but something was jamming it. Atticus searched Aida's eyes.

"No, Aida. You're free. Like you've always wanted to be. Whatever you have been through. It's gone. It's in the past, and as for now, you'll be safe once we get back to the Star Jumper," said Atticus.

Llub was scrambling to get the teleportation device working. Atticus was holding Aida's hand. They needed to take her back to the Star Jumper for a medical assessment.

"I have the teleportation device ready and working, Atticus," informed Llub.

Atticus took a quick look around the temple room. He knew the Kernanites would be back for me, and so would Ba'Gam. Atticus looked down as everything suddenly became illuminated and disappeared.

Once they reached the Star Jumper, Atticus brought Aida to the medical area of the Star Jumper. She laid her on a table. Her life signs were still erratic. Her hands were sweaty, and her hair was singed. Atticus retook a reading of Aida. What was happening to Adia's body was not known to the Star Jumper's medical database.

Atticus took further scans and looked through the medical database for more information about the medical knowledge of the Humars. When he did a deep scan of Aida's body, another life sign appeared on the sensors: She was pregnant.

Atticus was not sure how to take the news. He knew he must continue to attend to Aida, though. Llub slowly piloted the Star Jumper away from Xo'Ti. Aida finally woke briefly.

"What happened? This…this… I'm afraid that's not right," she said.

"You're on the Star Jumper right now. And you're pregnant," Atticus stated.

"I'm what…but the ritual…. the call…the Kernanites…Didn't they know?" she said.

Atticus felt anger go through his body. He needed more knowledge of the Kernanites and Aida's species; hours passed as Atticus poured over texts in the database of the Star Jumper. What he found about Aida and the Humar stunned him. It seemed the Humar have an ancestral urge to sacrifice themselves once they encounter aggression or the possibility of death. The Kernanites met the Humars long ago. As far as Atticus could tell, there was an almost unknown relationship between Kernanites and the Humar to most of the galaxy.

Humars once—and still apparently—sacrifice themselves. However, the process was stopped. Atticus could only surmise it was because she was pregnant. The care for the baby inside her took over her body, her spirit, and her instinctual urges.

Atticus needed to tell Llub, so he did. His response was as a typical Itor would say, given the circumstances and what they had been through. He went over and took Aida's hand.

"He'll be a fighter, Aida," said Llub. His name will be known throughout the galaxy. He already has a good father, and you will make a wonderful mother." Llub returned to the pilot's chair and positioned the Star Jumper to enter hyperspace.

VIII

Atticus was still in the back of the Star Jumper with Aida when Llub called him over to the command module. The Star Jumper was in a region of space called the Barrens to Llub's species, Atticus found out a while ago. In the Barrens, a hyperdrive may have trouble keeping its power. Atticus looked through the command module window and then went to the operations and science consoles of the Star Jumper.

The Star Jumper had been picking up a lot of communications from around the galaxy, but nothing exciting or urgent. Atticus's knowledge of the stars was somewhat lacking. He had plenty of star maps but did not have time to study them. He hoped Llub knew what he was doing.

After going above the galaxy's plane, Llub called in Atticus again. He huffed and pointed at a medium-sized group of stars, then smiled.

"This is where I am from, Atticus, the Vador IV star system. And the homeworld of the Itors, Vinosa, is in the middle of the group of stars," explained Atticus.

"So, I take it we are heading to Itor space then," said Atticus.

"Yes, now that we are above the plain of the Barrens," stated Llub. "How is Aida?"

Llub knew that, at times, Atticus did not want to talk about Aida after the tragedy of what happened with the Kernanites. Atticus stared into space. Llub was a decent companion, but he knew there could be trouble.

"Alright, I'll go check up on Aida, and then we'll set a course for Vinosa," Atticus said excitedly.

The Star Jumper powered up and began its journey without a sound. Atticus slept next to Aida most nights and took care of her during the days to Vinosa. It took several rotations of the moons around Atticus's home planet of Stie Lux to get to Vinsoa.

When they entered the Vado IV solar system, Aida started to sit up in bed. She looked bewildered. She shielded her eyes from the lights of the Star Jumper.

"Where are we?" she said.

"We are in the Vado IV star system in Itor space. It's the home star system of Vinosa," explained Atticus.

"How did we make it here?" said Aida in a state of confusion.

"Well, we made it through the experience with some luck," smirked Atticus.

A light went on in the back of the Star Jumper, signaling to Atticus that the Star Jumper had entered orbit around Vinosa. Atticus went up to the command module. He sat in the co-pilot's chair. Llub seemed more relaxed now that space docking was underway.

Llub communicated that they need a space for ground transport. After a while, the three were on the space dock orbiting Vinosa. To Aida and Atticus, it was a wonder to see so many Itors in one place at one time. They were a mighty species, and they achieved wonders.

They found a space for ground transport. They were to head to one of the Itorian cities for scientific research on Vinosa. Llub had decided Aida would benefit from Itorian medical and physical science. Aida got up from the table as the transport touched down.

Vinosa was a wind-swept world with notoriously unreliable weather patterns. Its arid environment was dotted with rain clouds as Atticus looked out over a cliff not far from the city of Dowa. Scientists quickly emerged from the buildings surrounding the landing pad. They promptly took Aida and put her on a floating table. Atticus and Llub followed them.

While walking, Atticus suddenly experiences an intense headache. His eyes became sensitive to the light of the buildings and the sun. For a moment, he thought he would go blind. Atticus briefly fell to the ground, only to be propped up by Llub.

"What happened?" said Llub.

"I don't know. It's nothing, just a slight headache," murmured Atticus under his breath. His hands were becoming sweaty as well. Aida was taken inside a building that looked like a hospital. Atticus decided to stay outside. He avoided the Itors. He did not want them to ask him questions. The headache and palm sweating remained.

Llub stood outside the building with Atticus. Itors occasionally buzzed around them. They had a meeting with one of the generals in the Itorian military. After the loss of Captain Bahm and the fights with the Kernanites, they needed backup to help them cross to the Independent Worlds. An Itor dressed in a silver jumpsuit approached them.

"Llub of the Fifth Covenant. I'm Grand General Rowber. Nice to meet you again," said the Grand General Rowber.

"The same with you, Grand General of the Fleet," exclaimed Llub.

"This is my companion, Atticus Lokar," stated Itor.

"Glad to meet you. What could a Grand General do for you two?" said the Grand General.

The Grand General, Llub, and Atticus went to an area of Dowa where most of the Itorian fleet was stationed. Atticus was amazed at how advanced some of their technology was. One Itorian ship could take on three old Kernanite ships. He was not sure about the new Kernanite ships he had seen. Llub was inside one of the vessels when an Itorian female scream was heard. He and the Grand General stepped outside the vessel.

Something happened to Atticus. Atticus had covered his eyes. His exposed skin had black tendrils going through it. Some Itors went over to assist Atticus, but suddenly, light emanated from Atticus, and it threw the Itors to the floor. Atticus was on the ground in the area with the Itorian Fleet. Any object that was not attached to something began to float. The Itors brought out their scanners and ion pistols until Llub approached them.

"Lower your weapons. Whatever happened to Aida has also now happened to Atticus," he stated.

The black tendrils continued to course through his skin. Llub managed to comfort Atticus by putting his hand on his shoulder, but objects were still flying everywhere in the military field of Dowa. Llub did not step back from the powerful force coming from Atticus.

Atticus started to moan and scream. Then, lighted matter shot out of his hands. It hit Llub and sent him reeling to the other side of the military center. Members of the Itorian fleet took a step back. As soon as they did, Atticus looked up to the sky and screamed angrily. The pulsating light emanating from Atticus went up through the windy sky into space.

What the Itors saw after frightened them. Blue ether, like the Kernanites, had come from Atticus' eyes. His skin was sprayed with black lines. Some lead to and from his organs. Atticus stood there with a clenched fist as if he was about to take on the Itors around him. Llub started to come for Atticus even with the energy coursing through Atticus.

The Itors continue to step back from Atticus and murmur amongst themselves. Atticus pulled himself together but felt like whatever had happened to him, he had already won. As soon as Atticus saw the Grand General, he thought of Aida immediately.

He signaled to Llub that they needed to find Aida. Llub was stunned at his companion's request. The blackened vessels of his skin bulging out and pulsating.

"Atticus, you are not well!" said Llub.

"I won't have anyone see me until we get to the Independent Worlds," stated Atticus firmly.

Whatever Atticus had gone through was beginning to fade away from the memory of the Itors standing around Atticus. When Llub looked directly into Atticus's eyes, blue flashed from them. Llub brushed it off like the rest of the Itors. They had called Atticus a friend and knew he was far from home. And, he had met the enemy. Or, at least, they thought.

Atticus and Llub hurried to the medical center where Aida was being treated. Before they got to her room, she was standing at the doorways.

She smiled. Her crystal white skin was shining again. She was wearing an Itor jumpsuit.

Atticus and Aida hugged immediately. *Did she know what just happened to him?* About fifteen doctors were approaching Atticus, Llub, and Aida.

"How did she do, doctors? Do you know what happened to her," said Atticus in a firm yet worried voice.

"There's a lot more to discover in this galaxy or more precisely in this universe," said one doctor.

"Aida was a tough patient. We do not know much about the Humar—medically speaking," said another.

"But, we do know it increased the speed of her metabolism," stated a young doctor.

They all examined Atticus from head to toe. His body was still dotted with black vessels, and the Itors did not look comfortable.

In the background, Grand General Rowber looked like he was still fulfilling his promise of gathering some ships for Atticus and the group to take to the Independent Worlds. Adia looked Atticus over at the changes that had suddenly happened to him. She nodded her head in approval.

"This Atticus was supposed to happen," she said as she pointed at the black veins.

An Itorian fighter ship landed a short distance from them. Adia congratulated Llub and Atticus for brokering a deal with the Itors. Llub looked over the fighter ship.

"I can't wait to get this into space," he said.

"I can. It would be nice to have another person who can pilot," quipped Atticus.

Atticus stood by the Itorian fighter ship talking to Llub. Aida, meanwhile, returned to the ground for space transport. When she managed to find a place to sit, she mused at everything that had happened. *This is how it is supposed to happen*, she thought. She knew there was more to Atticus. *After all, what was a Stie Luxian doing on Fina and then managed to pick up a female Humar? Who is he?* she thought.

Llub boarded onto the Itorian fighter. Atticus waved back at him. Atticus still needed Llub but needed even more, considering the life-altering events. He boarded the ground-to-space transport.

When they reached the space dock, Atticus felt more relieved that nothing else had happened. Aida, too, looked more than thankful. They intend now to head directly in the direction of the Independent Worlds. There was not much on the way to Atticus's home world except for an old Stie Luxian colony on Ui-Jer.

Ui-Jer was not just a colony; it was also known as a fun place to stop and engage in plenty of entertainment activities. It was a world dotted with islands and lacked a main continent. It was a mid-way point where Llub and Atticus could sequence their engines correctly.

Llub was already at the space dock by the time the ground-to-space transport. Atticus entered the space dock and tipped one of the assistants watching over the Star Jumper. The Star Jumper gently separated from the space dock with a low rumble. When they were past the rings of Vinosa, they jumped into hyperspace.

Atticus stared at the darkness of space and then looked at the blackness of his veins. Aida was sleeping in the passenger module of the Star Jumper. It took about one rotation of a Stie Luxian day to reach Ui-Jer. Llub arrived promptly on time as well. The three went through the protocols of onboarding and boarding. Their space-to-ground transport reached one of the far-flung archipelagos of Ui-Jer.

As soon as they disembarked the space-to-ground transport, they were plummeted into mayhem. The locals were having a ritual called Manertom. It was a celebration of love and freedom. It was something the three were looking for—especially freedom. Some of the locals started to stare at Atticus and his group. Gossip looked like it was spreading. Wind swept through Atticus's hair, flung his hood back, and revealed his humanness. The locals were shocked he was a fellow Stie Luxian.

Aida and Llub walked with Atticus along the community near the beach on Ui-Jer. They decided to walk along the coast, and the wind swept through the orange sand of the island. After they strode along the coast, they returned to the community where they had arrived.

Some locals looked over their shoulders, and others pointed at Atticus, Llub, and Aida. As they were on the main street, a middle-aged local approached them. He suddenly raised his fist and sent it flying to punch Atticus. Atticus moved out of the way of the punch.

"What's your problem?" said Atticus.

"You are a traitor who left the home world," said the man.

"I don't even know you," Atticus reproached.

Atticus thought for a moment. Technically, no one in this colonial world knew who he was. This man seemed to. And he was angry.

"Your mother was a noble queen from D'Er—one of the Independent Worlds which was a member of the Council," said the man.

Atticus was immediately flooded with emotions. *With such a strange accusation, how could Llub and Aida believe Atticus?* he thought. He never thought it was worthwhile to bring his past up to people he has met in his travels unless the situation warranted it. He wanted to know more of what this man knew.

"First, what's your name?" Atticus said quizzically

"My name is Goronoi of Ui-Jer. I lived here on Ui-Jer and was taught the ways of the Independent Worlds by my mother and father," he clamored.

Atticus still could not believe he was about to bring up this past this close to returning to Stie Lux. Atticus looked the man up and down. The sun shone on the man's black hair.

"So, your family was not originally from an Independent World? Then, how do you know my mother was a queen from D'Er?" Atticus inquired further.

"My family sought protection from the Independent Worlds when the Kernanites went on their most recent military campaign over thirty years ago. My father became a member of your mother's diplomatic civil servants," he said.

Aida and Llub looked at him with concern as Atticus affirmed with the man. Suddenly, Goronoi bowed and closed his eyes. Atticus recognized the movement as a sign of respect for someone who has passed on to the afterlife.

"Your father was one of the great generals during the last war. He has always been spoken well here on Ui-Jer," said Goronoi.

Atticus wanted to know why Goronoi threw a punch at him. He was a fellow Stie Luxian. The ridges on his brow proved that he was, but Atticus looked slightly different from him. Goronoi saw this and attempted to touch Atticus on the arm. He was repulsed.

Atticus looked at Aida, who looked like she was absorbing the man's words. Atticus wanted to know how people would perceive him and what that could mean to his search for freedom.

IX

G oronoi continued to size up Atticus. The group of three stood in front of the lonely local of Ui-Jer. Finally, Atticus moved.

Goronoi countered Atticus's movement, but not before Atticus could build up more strength and send the local to the floor. The fighting surprised Aida, and the accusations Goronoi made about Atticus.

Llub helped to pin the local to the ground. The local had a muscular build, so his strength started to overtake Atticus, but not with the strength of an Itor. They finally got Goronoi's hands behind his back. Llub held him in place.

"What kind of fight do you have with me?" said Atticus to Goronoi.

"A fight for honor and truth," huffed Goronoi.

"What do you know about my family, my mother and father?" said Atticus.

"I know pretty much everything," said Goronoi. "You might as well kill me with my intentions for taking you prisoner."

Atticus was bewildered. *Who was this guy?* he thought. Stie Luxians never fought each other, and the Council has held the Independent Worlds together for millennia. Goronoi looked at Atticus again.

"And you look different. You're—not a Stie Luxian anymore—only an impression of a Stie Luxian," said Goronoi.

"You might stop wanting to take me prisoner," instructed Atticus. "Thank you for your testimony about my family, but I'm returning to Stie Lux. Everything is fine for now."

Some of the locals—who were loyal to the Independent Worlds—came back to take Goronoi. Atticus felt exhausted from the fight. He tried to push thoughts of traitors in the back of his mind. He wanted to enjoy his time on Ui-Jer, but this was serious.

Llub started asking some locals whether they had seen any black, skinned Kernanites. They then pointed to Atticus and his blackened veins. They had seen this long ago in the history of Ui-Jer.

Llub returned, worried from questioning the locals. He wrote everything down, and then he began to tell Atticus what he had found.

"They said you are a Kernanite, Atticus," said Llub with some dismay.

"What do you mean? We already fought them. We know they are on our trail. They even kidnapped Aida. I'm no Kernanite!" shouted Atticus.

Llub looked at Atticus and Aida. Itors were formidable in their knowledge of the galaxy, but this tested their power and prowess. It seemed like Llub still trusted Atticus. Atticus looked at Llub closely as well. Llub broke the silence.

"When we were on Vinosa, the best scientists took a while to figure out what was happening to Aida from a scientific perspective. And, now, you, Atticus," he said convincingly.

Llub appeared to search his mind for an answer. The Itors were a powerful race, but they lacked grace and wisdom. He thought deeply.

"It must be a spiritual or religious event," he said.

Atticus looked at Llub. That is what the Ui-Jerian local was trying to say. As far as the locals were concerned, Atticus was a Kernanite, but he was not just any relation to a Kernanite.

"Are you the son of a queen and a general?" said Llub.

Atticus's eyes gave Llub a piercing look, "I am who I say I am, and until I say anything more, that guy does not matter."

Llub looked at Aida. Aida did not help with a conclusion on Atticus's condition. Llub looked concerned about both Aida and Atticus.

Suddenly, Atticus grabbed his upper right arm. He wailed in pain. Aida and Llub rushed over. Atticus kept screaming. They tore off his jacket. His tattoo was glowing.

All Stie Luxians had a tattoo indicating they were a part of the Independent Worlds and named their family. Llub and Aida could not decipher what it meant or said. Atticus looked down at his tattoo. He could not believe his body reacted like it was to the metal in the tattoos.

Llub got a medical kit to look over Atticus's shoulder. Aida stood watching. The ointments from the medical kit soothed Atticus's tattoo, but it was still glowing, and Atticus was still in pain.

Darkness was falling on Ui-Jer, and they needed to make camp. They found a local Ui-Jerian loyal to the Independent Worlds and camped by the beach in one of their bungalows.

Aida stood on a rock. She looked out to sea. The starry night above the crashing waves was astonishing. Llub walked up to Aida, and a meteor flew past in the atmosphere. The Ui-Jerian moon shone a red glow on the sands of the archipelago. Atticus was in the bungalow, tending to his arm.

Suddenly, he heard a ringing in his ear, and the inside of the bungalow went dark. He listened to the haunting sounds of someone speaking, and his eyes darted from side to side in the dark.

"Who's there? What do you want with me?" shouted Atticus. He heard the muffled sounds of someone's voice, and Atticus's tattoo glowed even brighter. He heard someone calling his name.

Atticus only felt an ominous feeling until he suddenly felt like someone was inside his head. Images of Aida flashed by him and himself. He saw the Kernanite home world, then nothing.

Then, a group of letters looked like they were burned into the darkness. Bright red and orange embers fell from the letters. Atticus squinted. It said, "T'Shar." Atticus stood before the letters, and suddenly, something or someone grabbed him by the neck. His feet were lifted from the floor so much that he could look down at the bungalow floor. He kept looking down, and then the bright, blue flame of a Kernanite's eyes came into view.

"You don't need to retraumatize me, you know," he said to the Kernanite.

Suddenly, a cold wind blew over him even though he was on a warm beach in Ui-Jer. Atticus looked around again as the room went pitch black. A roar was heard like waves crashing on a beach. Then, light broke through the black, and the silhouette of a Kernanite was there. It wielded a sword with stars seen in it.

"I know who you are," said Atticus, "You're the Kernanite Ba'Gam."

The figure nodded and beckoned to Atticus. He felt a mysterious attraction. He could not help but get closer to the Kernanite even though he knew he could kill him. For some reason, Atticus felt the Kernanite was trying to show him something.

A star map popped up between the Kernanite and him. It showed all the constellations of every region of the galaxy. Atticus looked for the Independent Worlds, and he found them. He found Stie Lux, the multicolored sphere, spinning in space slowly. The Kernanite waved over the map, showing distant Humarian space. Several constellations were highlighted. In some of the worlds, the constellations had not been inhabited for centuries or millennia or had never been inhabited at all. However, they shared one thing: a group of comets always passed by them. There was a total of twelve comets.

Atticus noticed some of the comets were getting close to Ui-Jer and Stie Lux and the Independent Worlds. Another one was near Kernanite Space. The Kernanite then looked at Atticus.

"Where is the Humar?" said the Kernanite.

Atticus was puzzled. *Couldn't he see her?* Atticus's eyes darted around the darkness.

"Can't you see her?" he said.

The Kernanite glared at him. "Her telepathic abilities are hindering me."

"What do you want with her?" demanded Atticus.

"I want a sacrifice to renew the life cycles of my race," said the Kernanite. "There must be a sacrifice from the lesser races."

Atticus did not know what he was talking about, but he knew the Kernanite was referring to the current makeup of the galaxy. The Kernanite pointed over to the homeworld of the Humar. In seconds, ghastly scenes of cities burning and people fleeing were shown. He then pointed over to Stie Lux. He could see him and Aida with a baby. Atticus and her were in the city, in one of his ancestral homes—one of his father's.

Then she saw Aida running and giving the baby to the servant. In an instant, Kernanites broke through the doors of Aida's room, and a gun hit her, and she fell wounded. Atticus clenched his fists.

"NOOOOOO!" he said to the Kernanite. "Why did you show me that?"

"To show you the way," said the Kernanite. "You are one of us, son of T'Shar."

"What are you talking about?" exclaimed Atticus, "Who are the T'Shar?"

"You are fortunate, Atticus," said the Kernanite Ba'Gam, "You have the gift of bringing the enemy close." The Kernanite smiled.

"Your mother and father kept you from knowing your true identity. You remember your childhood, don't you? You remember the loss of your father during the last war and your mother to the pandemic," stated the Kernanite.

"They were no fools when they brought you into this life, Atticus. Unfortunately, neither am I nor my race. I want something from you, Atticus," he said ominously.

"What do you want, Ba'Gam? And whatever you want, you cannot have. It's mine," exclaimed Atticus.

"Oh?" said Ba'Gam powerfully.

Suddenly, Atticus's eyes started to glow, and so did the tattoo on his right arm. The Kernanite Ba'Gam was lifting him from the floor. Atticus looked down over the star map.

"What I want from you…Is something…more precious than life itself," said Ba'Gam sinisterly.

A knife suddenly was at Atticus' throat. Atticus tried to free himself of the grip that Ba'Gam had on him. Ba'Gam moved the knife away from Atticus.

"You are indeed scared, Atticus Lokar of the D'Ner and First Royal of the Independent Worlds," said Ba'Gam lucidly.

Atticus could not see the Kernanite Ba'Gam since he was hooded. He struggled to keep himself standing. Atticus touched his right arm. It was still glowing, and everything around him was still dark.

"What do I want from you, Atticus? I want the life of the Humar," said Kernan explicitly, "This one is brave, and I can feel her!"

"You can't have her," said Atticus.

"But you don't even know how special you are, Atticus. You are the son of the T'Shar, who was brought into this life to make a choice. A choice which has fallen on the side of the Kernanites and into the fate of many" said Ba'Gam.

Atticus could not stop thinking what the Ba'Gam was thinking. He hid his identity, which was true. *How did the Kernanite know so much? he thought.* He sensed a weakness in the Kernanite's plot.

"I may not need you, Atticus, but I need the Humar. I need a sacrifice of innocence. You are the T'Shar Atticus chosen by the gods. You are to make a choice. And I can tell you what choice you will make. You will choose the side of us, the ancient race called the Kernanite. You will give us the Humar friend as sustenance. It will be not one life but two," said Ba'Gam.

Atticus heard someone in the bungalow. Then, the darkness gradually disappeared, and the figure of the Kernanite disappeared into the moonlight. Atticus' eyes met Aida's. She grabbed him and brushed the sweat off his brow. Llub was with Aida.

"What is it, Atticus?" said Aida.

"A Kernanite…The Kernanite Ba'Gam came…and said I must do something in their name…or…or…"

Atticus began to lose consciousness. Some of the locals ran in to see if they could help. They also sensed a presence to confirm what Atticus was saying. Llub grabbed Atticus and placed him on a cot in the bungalow. Aida knelt by the cot and tended to Atticus. Atticus' tattoo was still glowing, but Aida covered it so the locals would not see it.

Atticus was despondent. He was pushing Llub away and some of the locals and screaming at them. He reached until he saw Aida.

"Aida! Aida! I thought I lost you! I could have sworn I went through with it," he said.

Aida knelt beside Atticus. Atticus was breathing heavily. Aida used some of her telepathic abilities to deduce what he was experiencing—some induced trauma.

"But the baby!" Aida lamented.

"The Kernanites can't have him. I won't let them," screamed Atticus.

Aida touched his temples, and immediately, Atticus stopped breathing so heavily. Atticus got up and sat on the right side of the cot. *This was getting hard to keep a secret,* he thought. He decided not to tell Llub and Aida what had happened since he could not comprehend it. Atticus had only vaguely remembered how he had lost his mother so long ago. He felt like he was losing someone close to him again. And he was losing Aida fast.

He thought of everything. He thought about how they had found the Chalice of Life together and had gone to all these worlds. *How could it be he would lose her?* Atticus touched her stomach. He could feel the warmth of another life. He sharply took his hand away when he noticed an unwelcoming feeling. *How could he tell Aida and Llub he is from an ancient race as ancient as the Kernanites named the T'Shar?*

Atticus looked around the bungalow and laid back in bed. The locals went back to their camps. And Llub sang a traditional Itorian epic, which soothed Atticus. Aida made her bed beside Atticus and then gradually fell asleep. Llub stayed awake, sleeping until the moon was high in the night sky.

At the space dock orbiting Ui-Jer, there was a rush to the command center. Hyperspace signatures had been detected in the distance. Whoever they were, they were already right on top of the space dock, thought a crewman.

The space dock crew members attempted to contact the area where the hyperspace signatures were detected. They summoned their captain. Several Kernanite warships were spotted.

The captain of the space dock called all his men to duty. As Ui-Jer was spinning and sleeping, Kernanite warships were seen in Independent World territory for the first time in centuries. The crewman flew their craft to the warships. Something strange occurred, though. It was as if the warships were sleeping. Their power was minimal, and the command center was blocked from their communication channels. That was until one space dock fighter decoded a message a Kernanite warship was sending. It was a message of not peace or war. It was a message for help.

X

The space dock crew members and fighters were baffled by this message for help. The Kernanite warships were careening towards them. The crew of the space dock scrambled to get all dock ships away from the space dock.

When the last ship left the space dock, a Kernanite warship crashed into the dock, igniting an explosion that could be seen from the ground on Ui-Jer. The blast was heard across the archipelago where Llub, Aida, and Atticus were.

Nobody had a chance to get some sleep. The locals were pointing and looking at the night sky or running, screaming, and taking what they could from their houses. The fiery remnants of the Kernanite warship reigned down from orbit.

Atticus grabbed his chest and crawled his way out of the bungalow. *Was it already time for the Kernanite's words to come true?* Fire exploded above the water and danced on the waves away from the beach. Atticus, Aida, and Llub looked over the water to the horizon. Explosions and fire could be seen in large areas. Llub brought out his communicator.

"Llub to Space Dock Ui-Jer!" said Llub.

Nothing was heard on the other side except the ping of a location finder. Moments passed and then minutes. The group assumed the worst. Nobody survived, and the Star Jumper was destroyed.

A leader from one of the villages by the beach ran up to Atticus,

"Was that the space dock?" said the frightened villager.

"Yes, it unfortunately was. Nobody made it out. We lost our transport, the Star Jumper," said Atticus.

Llub ran over to a bungalow to signal that they survived the crashing landing of the space dock. Atticus grabbed Aida and pulled her away from the brightening light of the crash landing. The excellent beach air hit his tattoo. The behavior of the tattoo meant Kernanites were coming. Flames flickered over the beach, and Atticus continued to look out to sea.

"Come on, Atticus!" said Llub, "They found the Star Jumper."

A crewman from the space dock was standing somberly outside the village limits at a landing pad. Some medical personnel were attending some of the space dock crew. Atticus searched the beach to see if he could find Aida. Llub and Atticus stumbled on the back of the Star Jumper. A crewman was piloting the craft now. In the panic of the crash, Atticus felt the Ba'Gam had won. *Did he also know that Aida has a child on the way? Why did it have to be Aida? It could be any other Humar in the galaxy. Two lives were at stake now.*

Atticus searched his mind for an answer as to the next move of the Ba'Gam. Glimpses of the future passed before Atticus. He wanted to change what Ba'Gam had said about Aida. He tried to touch Aida and prayed that what happened was just a nightmare. He felt the cool beach air on his face again. As the Star Jumper door closed, he looked at Aida, nodding back and forth through sleep.

He wanted to run away from it all. He felt like a coward for letting Ba'Gam discover Aida. He should have done more to protect her. Now, they're running and need more alliances. Images flashed before Atticus's mind. Fire, screams, and his mother holding him close to her body. He held on to a necklace with his family's crest on it. His mother and he were taken to an underground complex where they could escape.

He remembers his mother as the most elegant woman in the known galaxies. She was like a dream, always there to comfort him against the sharpness of his era and barren space. His father was there when he was young. He was the shelter under which Atticus transformed and prospered. Atticus also remembers the fateful day when his father was called to duty to defend their home. He hears the murmurs of the servants consoling his grandmother when his father tells the family of an impending attack, and he wants to serve them with honor.

Some of the servants cried when they were told some of them were to leave since an attack may come, but all that was so long ago, Atticus continued to think. Atticus believed they could only go back to one place, Stie Lux. They must go there now before the situation gets out of hand.

Aida still had the secret of their unborn child. A future Atticus could see who lay within her. The Kernanites want to eliminate his child. He felt like his world was ending. The Kernanites found something special in Atticus. Atticus thought the universe was crafting something against him. He felt like Ba'Gam had touched something in him, something ancient. It was harder to contain ever since the war with the Kernanites started. He felt like he was a liar. It was harder to see the truth now that his secret was known.

He buried the secret deep inside him and covered his life with lies. So much so that he wished the dead bury the dead—his mother and father included. Aida looked peaceful there, lying asleep on the back of the Star Jumper. He went to the other end of the Star Jumper. Atticus could not get the image of one of the complexes back on Stie Lux that he and his mother and father hid in during the attacks on their home world. Atticus felt he wanted Aida and the power shown by the Kernanites.

He felt like he somehow knew the Kernanites. Nobody seemed ready to admit what happened to Atticus, Aida, and Llub. And, now, it seemed the rest of the galaxy. The Star Jumper continued its way to Stie Lux. Twisted space passed before the windows of the Star Jumper. It felt like centuries since the events of Xo'Ti and their journey. And, now, this. Atticus needed a haven. He thought quickly—the *asteroids of the Devlin XX star system.* The asteroids of Devlin XX were the harbors of a race known as Jael. That race is known for thought, planning, and strategy. They had long secluded themselves among the rock and ice of Delvin XX. The Jael had fought back countless invasions of their territory.

Llub was at the console piloting the Star Jumper. Atticus' tattoo continued to glow. It altered Atticus to the fact that Kernanites were nearby or following them. Atticus went to the communications console and attempted to retrieve the deteriorated message for help sent through space.

Atticus grabbed a cup of *gar'kirtori—or Stie Luxian tea*—and thought about Captain Reno. The possibility that the message could have been from him. Atticus pondered more about Reno. Even though Atticus was worried, Reno was a trained warrior and soldier. He would know where to go to find Atticus. He spent more time analyzing the broken message until he fell asleep at the console.

Atticus awoke to the Star Jumper shaking. He looked around the command center. The pilot's chair was empty. He went back to the passenger's capsule and found Llub asleep. He punched him on the shoulder. Llub's skin and body absorbed the punch, and instead, Atticus wailed in pain. Itors were indeed a strong race. Atticus decided to shout in his ear instead, figuring it would surprise him enough to coax him back to piloting the Star Jumper. Itors liked surprises in their interactions and culture.

"What was that for?" said Llub.

"You left the pilot's console and fell asleep, and now the Star Jumper is going through turbulence," commanded Atticus.

Llub got up from the bed and brushed himself off. He furrowed his brow with concern. The Star Jumper continued to shake. He ran up to the command center. They had finally reached the asteroids of Delvin XX. The forward sensors would guide the Star Jumper through the outermost asteroid field to where the Jaelians built their refuge.

The communications consoled beeped and hissed. The Star Jumper was picking up another message with an encryption code resembling the Star Jumper's code. *How is that possible?* Atticus thought. Every Star Jumper had a unique encryption code. Atticus decided to decode it. The code was in a language he did not understand, but he recognized the voice saying the code. It was Captain Reno Bahm. He was alive. Or was he? On Ui-Jer, whoever was in pursuit or pursuing ended up crashing.

Llub motioned to Atticus. They both gazed out the window. They had reached the innermost asteroids. Sunlight bounced off the ice-covered craters on the largest asteroids. Atticus, Aida, and Llub could see the gleaming biospheres of Delvin XX. The piloting console signaled to a space dock. Atticus held Aida's hand. In the reflection of the glass of the Star Jumper's view screen, he could see his tattoo still glowing. Aida had recovered from the incident on Ui-Jer. Atticus went further than holding her hands and touched her belly. He wondered how long it would be until the child was here. The Humar is so different than the rest—ancient and mysterious.

The crew of three entered the central biosphere of the Jaelians. There was no one around them when they entered the biosphere. The Jaelian race was split between those who lived on the surface of asteroids and those who lived beneath their surfaces. Aida showed concern, but it was not an overt concern for their arrival on the asteroids of Devlin XX.

Several holes opened up around and in front of Aida, Llub, and Atticus. A robotic-looking creature with appendages like a spider emerged smoothly from hibernation. A brain pulsated in the forehead region of the robot. It was part organic and part machine. Its bulbous eyes looked glaringly back at the three of them.

Aida touched her stomach. The robot had a screen on its chest next to its spidery arms. The three stood before it, and a hum came from it. A laser fell on Aida's stomach. The robot's screen lit up with the words *house* and *family.* Llub drew an ion gun from his hip. Atticus motioned him to lower the weapon.

"It seems to know what has happened," said Atticus.

"It's scanning us. We should shoot it!" exclaimed Llub.

The robotic thing backed away from the three of them and walked into the distance of the dome-shaped biosphere. The biosphere architecture was old and sophisticated, and the Jaelians had not changed their taste for centuries.

They walked to the other side of the biosphere, and a door opened. At first, it did not move. Then, Aida moved her hand above the door. It opened. Atticus looked quizzically at her. *She was practicing more,* he thought. The door opened slowly, showing a shadowy room with windows in the darkness of space. Towards the end of the room was a viewing area. Aida walked to the viewing area first. Aida looked out upon a gigantic crater in the asteroid that seemed endless. In what seemed like the middle of the crater was a cylinder hovering above the crater with skeletons carved into its surface. There was a long causeway to the cylinder.

"Come on," said Aida, "We need to get closer."

Gusts of air whipped past them as they walked to the other side of the causeway. Once they reached the cylinder, Atticus took out a scanner. His brow furrowed. He plugged in more information.

"It's old. And, those are Humarian inscriptions," Atticus said in a growlingly hushed whisper.

Atticus' eyes darted around and back and forth. Fast-moving air whipped around them again. Llub's purple eyes analyzed the structure.

"Those are reliefs of Humar skeletons," said Llub, "It looks like the Jaelians have lived up to their name about hiding things."

Atticus touched the cylinder and the inscriptions along it. Blue energy and pulsating light lit up the cylinder's inscriptions and slowly rotated. The tattoo on Atticus' arm also lit up, but it burned inside his skin this time. The cylinder opened fully, and inside was a tiara. Inscribed beneath where they laid were ancient sayings in Humaric writing.

The tiara was pure white. All three of them stood in awe. Aida touched Atticus' arm.

"It's like something I've seen only in a dream," said Aida.

"And it's meant for you," said an enigmatic voice behind them.

Aida whirled around, and there stood Captain Reno Bahm. She gasped. Atticus and Llub grabbed their ion guns.

"We thought you were dead, on the run, or in jail," said Atticus, visibly shaken.

Captain Reno Bahm shook his finger at Atticus and eyed the group. Bahm's face looked slightly more tired but in a sleeker uniform. He had his other hand behind his back while pointing and shaking his finger at Atticus.

"You just tricked the galaxy, son," Bahm told Atticus.

"I did no tricks, Bahm," retorted Atticus.

"And, lovely Aida. She found it was special after all," charmed Bahm snidely, "But there's more."

"The Star Union forgave me of my past and wants something in return. They want you, Aida, and we could throw in Atticus and Llub for kicks," snarled Bahm.

"Why does the Star Union want me, Bahm? I have done nothing wrong. I am free. If anything, I belong back to Fina. I am free. The Star Union does not occupy Fina," said Aida pridefully.

"Or, does it?" said Bahm, "The Kernanites have advanced into the Star Union's space, the Itors, and other regions. Pretty soon, they will be on top of the Independent Worlds and have their prizes—all three.

"A slave girl turned into a—" Bahm glanced at Aida, "Whatever."

"Shut up!" exclaimed Atticus. Atticus fired an ion shot at Bahm. Bahm stood firm, and a force shield absorbed the energy of the ion.

"You are going to regret doing that to me. I thought we could be friends. Do you want money, Atticus? A planet? We could give you all of it," said Bahm.

"She's not worth anything you could give," snapped Atticus again.

"Unfortunately, Atticus, the child, now belongs to the Star Union. For training as a weapon."

"He's no weapon," said Aida.

"I see. So, it's a boy," smiled Bahm, "He will be perceived as more powerful then."

Llub drew his ion gun and shot past Bahm's shoulder. Bahm countered and brought out a stunner gun and stunned him to the ground. Atticus jumped before Aida as Bahm shot a stunning ion ray at her. Atticus plummeted to the ground as he lost momentum from the jump. Aida grabbed the tiara and began running from Bahm. Bahm shook his head as the stunner gun charged again. He pointed it at Aida and fired it. He stunned her to the ground.

XI

Aida awoke holding Captain Bham's stunner gun. He lay beside Adia, and she listened for his breath to hear if he was dead or alive. His breath brushed her face softly. He was barely alive. A burn mark was scorched across his chest. Aida sat up and looked around the causeway. There was still no sign of the Jaelians. Llub and Atticus were unconscious on the floor.

A couple of feet away was the tiara from the cylinder. A weird feeling came over Aida. Suddenly, she felt anger and craved the air brushing against her face in the causeway. She grabbed the tiara and made her way to the center of the open cylinder. A case was there to place the tiara in it. And, on the case, there was an emblem she did not recognize. It was not the emblem of the Star Union, so she breathed a sigh of relief.

The inscriptions pulsated with light. Did *that* cause her failure to escape? It must have been the energy pulses because they also struck Bahm. It was simultaneous. As she hurried, she looked over the carnage caused by the mysterious energy from the cylinder. She looked for her med kit and other essentials to attend to Atticus and Llub. Before she could reach them, the lights went out in the biosphere and the causeway.

Aida looked around in fright. She turned on a light stick and waved it across the causeway and cylinder area. Suddenly, the light stick was struck from her hand, pouring out excess light, but it was enough to find the culprit. Dusty footprints maneuvered their way around Aida.

"Show yourself!" shouted Aida.

Aida stood straight up and grabbed another light stick. She could hear more feet. There was some audible chatter; she could tell it was the mysterious Jaelian language. One Jaelian appeared before Aida. Its purple-haired filled tentacle face and gazed at Aida with contempt and mercy. *No wonder they kept themselves cloaked and mysterious; they were hideous,* she thought. Despite her polite thought about the Jaelian, it decided to grab a staff from there and attempt to strike Aida. Instead, Aida caught the staff, embedded it into the causeway, and cracked it. Light scattered everywhere, revealing seven Jaelians. The sound of the staff striking the causeway was loud enough to push Llub and Atticus into consciousness.

Llub and Atticus held their heads, and each grabbed their respective wounds. As soon as Atticus came to, he set his ion gun into a levitation position to ion whip the Jaelians and was successful. The Jaelians' yellow blood oozed from his nose.

"What happened? The Jaelians are unconscious, and Bahm looks dead," said Llub.

"No, he is still living," confirmed Aida.

"Why did the Jaelians turn on us?" questioned Atticus.

"They are not like I remember them: peaceable, calm, and wise," lamented Llub.

"So, what do we do, guys? Go search for what happened with the Jaelians or retreat with Bahm," jousted Aida.

"Llub, you stay here with Bahm and the unconscious Jaelians. You know what to do if any of them wake back up. We will be fast," commanded Atticus. Beads of sweat dripped down Atticus's face. Aida looked determined as she ran alongside Atticus. Her crystal skin bounced the light the causeway and cylinder sent into the biosphere. They reached the door on one of the four causeways. One of those spidery, bulbous organic and inorganic robots from nowhere dropped down from the ceiling. Aida lifted her leg high and pounded her leg into the soft forehead of the robot. Liquid splattered onto Atticus and Aida. They hurried to the door. It opened quickly and quietly.

"What kind of room is this?" speculated Atticus.

"It looks like the room for a political person or a leader," stipulated Aida.

A chair in the room suddenly swiveled around to face Atticus and Aida. And, there was an uncloaked Jaelian in full, formal attire. It looked solemn.

"You thought you could run. You can't," said the Jaelian in a terse tone, "They will scour the galaxy and find your child, Aida, you, Llub, and even Captain Reno. The Jaelian Consortium now knows about the advancements of the Kernanites. You should seek shelter here or surrender. I am Mandz, by the way," said Mandz, putting his arms in his glittering robes.

The Jaelian's short tenacles on his face wiggled around and around with each breath from holes that served as nostrils. Two beady eyes continued to stare at Atticus and Aida. Mandz brought his hand up to his face and coughed. A watery substance from his tenacles dropped to the console he was sitting at.

"I've heard," said Mandz, "You want the baby for yourself, Aida."

Aida stiffened and let out a whimper. She felt a presence in her mind. Quickly, anger ran up her spine, and she lost control of her senses and body. A shockwave of energy zipped out of her body.

"Get out of my head!" said Aida, enraged at Mandz.

Atticus looked over the situation. The child was his as well. Atticus watched the two spar telekinetically. Suddenly, Aida was lifted in the air and then thrown to the floor. She let out another whimper.

"Stop, I don't want to fight you," commanded Atticus.

"Neither do I," said Mandz, "I also heard you are looking for a Chalice. A Chalice of Life. What do you think you would do with it? I hear you are headed for the Independent Worlds—Stie Lux. "

Atticus felt their plan was ripped away, but there was hope. Llub was still waiting for Atticus and Aida.

"Do you want it?" Atticus asked with a heavy breath. I could teleport it to you."

Atticus' body was tense and in a pouncing position. Mandz sat there with his arms crossed in his dazzling robes.

"Yes, I do. I'll give you some Jaelian coins. It's worth it. You'll see," affirmed Mandz.

Aida regained consciousness and stood up on her feet. She felt violated. *What happened?* She looked over at Atticus, who seemed unusually tired.

Mandz got up from his seat and waved Aida away. His robes waved in the air, and his tenacles left a puddle of ooze as he walked. Mandz felt over a controller pad and then looked at Atticus.

Atticus touched his utility belt to transport the Chalice of Life. Mandz gave him the coordinates, and Atticus pressed his belt to activate the teleportation device. The Chalice of Life appeared on a table about 50 feet from Mandz.

"You're giving him the Chalice!" exclaimed Aida.

"It will help protect our son, Aida. The Kernanites won't follow the Jaelians. They are too secretive and powerful," said Atticus hurriedly.

Atticus and Aida took some steps closer to Mandz. Some of his tentacles reached out to grab the Chalice by the neck. A strange hum filled the room. Then, the room was filled with bright blue light. The hum continued. Atticus and Aida looked at each other; now, they were standing on some starry, astral plane with Mandz.

Atticus and Aida could see Llub and the other Jaelians coming on the astral plane. In the distance, he could catch glimpses and sudden bursts of images of the advancements of the Kernanites into foreign territory. One world fell by another in the fire of weaponry from the Kernanites fleet. He could soon see some of the worlds of the Crinix Imperium taken by multiple fleets. Then, they were upon the Utopian Nebula. Atticus gulped while Aida's eyes flickered with fury. Llub ran over to them. Right before Llub, he saw the Itor homeworld filled with pockets of fire and his species retreating to some of the moons surrounding their homeworld.

The Jaelians walked up beside Atticus, Llub, and Aida. Mandz let the Chalice go, and it began to float. The astral plane focused on a giant, armored spaceship in the Kernanite fleet. They saw him—Ba'Gam. He stood before a massive invasion map of the galaxy. He was around some of his commanding officers. Something was different, though. A blue aurora surrounded Ba'Gam.

The commanding officers were attentive but seemed bothered by Ba'Gam. Everyone saw Ba'Gam's next move. He drew a line right to the Independent Worlds. The hum started again. It was as if the Chalice was trying to warn them of something. As quickly as the astral plane came, it disappeared.

Mandz gently turned around and faced everyone. He looked solemn and frightened. Someone could not mistake the secretive, stoical faces breaking under the stress of what they were shown today. The other Jaelians showed the same mix of emotions.

"What we saw today," said Mandz sadly, "confirmed the attacks on everyone. No more rumors or trickery. They want every world to fall by taking those worlds."

The other Jaliean went to the other side of the room and lined up behind Mandz. Looks of concern were everywhere. One intruded by tapping Mandz on his shoulder with his tentacle.

"What are we to do, Mandz?" said the Jaelian quizzically, "The Consortium may get hit next on Ba'Gam's list of targets. All our treasures lost; all our secrets lost. He'll find us like the Humar's child. Slowly like a predator stalking its prey."

Mandz massaged his tentacles with his left hand. The Chalice remained silent. He went over to a console and inputed some data. The Jaelian Consortium lacked a fleet, but they had advanced weaponry, which they traded on the market. The map did not show the Kernanites' advancements in their foreign territory; it was only a vision so far.

"I welcome Atticus, Aida, and Llub into the Jaelian Consortium. We will give them some of our technologies, information, and weaponry to help them fight the Kernanites. This is for the benefit of the Consortium and all Jaelians," stated Mandz firmly with the others.

"We have a lot of work to do then," chimed in Llub.

Adia gave an unforgiving look to Atticus. He waved him to the side of the group. And they huddled together.

"What do you think of the offer?" inquired Aida.

"I think they are being honest. They were just shown that their lives and way of life are at stake in this war," affirmed Atticus.

"Do you think they still want our child?" Aida questioned further.

Atticus raised his hand to calm Aida so the others would not hear their debate. Atticus noticed the bulge on Adia's belly. The child had grown inside of her. He was also worried about Llub. Llub saw the attack on the Itor homeworld.

Llub looked on at Aida and Atticus debating. His chest filled with grief as he remembered the images the Chalice presented before everyone. He felt threatened in a way at this revelation. *How did this strange object and the forces behind it know so much?* However, he knew at the same time it may be a great asset.

While Atticus and Aida were discussing things, Llub walked over to Mandz. The Jaelian was staring at the console at some military map, which caught Llub's eye. Llub gently coughed to grab the Jaelian's attention.

Mandz looked up, eyes wide in inquiry and secrecy. He rubbed his yellow and purple tentacles more and more. Llub was intrigued.

"An Itor? I forgot your kind were still in the galaxy. What is left of your species must mean Ba'Gram has been on the move for some time. I guess we didn't need the confirmation from the Chalice after all," wondered Mandz.

"We did," said Llub firmly. "The Chalice has proved decisive in the moments that it *worked*. What do you think the Chalice means? Where is it from? Can you determine anything about it?"

"The galaxy is older than you know," huffed Mandz, "Even you Itors who have started to leave the galax; you know that. You're too young to remember many of the teachings of your kind, eh? The Jaelian Consortium will search where the Chalice is from while we give you what you need, and you can stay as long as you want. Though our paths have crossed right now, you must leave quickly."

"I understand," Llub said, his head lowered in reverence for his kind and what the Jaelian said.

"Do you know where we began our journey, Mandz?" said Llub.

"No," said Mandz quickly.

"On Fina. An Outer World. I was there because I did not want to take the Great Migration with the other Itors. I took some friends, and that is how I met Atticus and everyone, including Captain Reno Bahm."

Mandz lifted an eyebrow and said, "I have heard of Fina. A bandit planet with potential. It has produced some heroes in its time, but it is not an old world like where you are headed on this journey."

"Fina is a world of hope. Aida was a slave girl there who sought freedom. Captain Reno was—well—in retirement. And Atticus was having fun."

The Itor looked puzzled momentarily as someone caught his attention out of the corner of his eye. Aida and Atticus had stopped conversing, and Atticus was walking over to Mandz. Mandz, too, saw what grabbed Llub's attention. Aida had gone to a window on the other side of the room that looked out over the biosphere and onto the asteroid. She was grabbing her stomach, and she looked like she was shimmering.

Atticus grabbed Llub by the arm. Llub shot a look at Atticus with his purple eyes. Concern riddled Atticus' face.

"Llub, it looks like we are learning more about the Humar. Aida's pregnancy may reach its end at any moment. It was revealed while we were debating the journey," informed Atticus.

The other Jaelians looked at Aida and began looking at her shimmering form. They pointed and laughed. Some even waged bets about what would happen next in this situation.

"You Humars, always putting on a show. No wonder they are another species without a homeworld. The child of a drifter that will be" said the Jaelian with a scar on his face near his tentacles.

"Maybe the child will be a new species. I heard it is a cross being the Stie Luxian and the Humar," laughed a Jaelian with a crest on his forehead.

Mandz suddenly drew his attention away from Llub and Atticus and looked at the other Jaelians. His tentacles started to lift, and three or four dart-sized objects shot from his mouth underneath his tentacles. The other Jaelians immediately fell on their faces.

"You fools! Haven't you seen a woman, regardless of their species, pregnant? Who knows what she will do? The child has our blessing. The Jaelian Consortium will provide for it," commanded Mandz to the now-tired Jaelians.

Atticus went over to Aida again and immediately wrapped his arms around her. They looked out the window, and Aida pressed her face against his.

Atticus felt the warmth of her body.

"Did you hear Aida?" he said with a loving whisper. "We have their blessing! So, we have more on our side on this journey."

XII

It had been 400 days since they saw water on the dunes of Y'Fert. Last night, Llub made camp tending to the remnants of a local animal the natives called a *hodit*. It was great for making tents, but they were torn to rags easily in the harsh winds of the planet's tempest weather. So every day, Llub went out to find more *hodit*. He even felt that the *hodit* knew that they were needed. It was their sacrifice.

During the cold nights on Y'Fert, the hides of the *hodit* warmed everyone and gave them a good sleep. Y'Fert was an unknown planet to the sojourners. *Hodit* were horse-like animals with three horns on their heads. Two on their forehead and one on their long nose. Horns also protrude from their massive shoulders. The location of the planet was revealed to them by the Jaelians on a map given to Atticus. Captain Bahm was taken prisoner and brought with them to work on a farm next to a river where the dunes gave way to an expansive plain.

One day, when Llub was on the dune, some natives—they call themselves the Pedisax or the Gatherers in Atticus' language—made their tents around a large *hodit* herd Llub was corralling. The Pedisax were six-legged species. Four legs descended like crab legs surrounding their bodies, while the other two were attached to a torso. Their face and heads were fierce. Various organisms grew on the faces of the Pedisax, drawing what moisture they could from their bodies. Their mouths had large pinchers used to eat insects and animals. The Pedisax welcomed Llub into their circle of tents around the *hodit*.

Llub entered one tent and encountered some Pedisax staring straight at a fire. Llub took his hand and waved it in front of them. Their eyes glistened in the fire, and their nostrils gently flared as they breathed in white smoke. A Pedisax was sitting in the corner of their massive tent with all six legs crossed, holding a staff and reading. Llub moved through the white smoke to the other side of the tent. As he looked at the Pedisax, he almost seemed blind. His fingers fumbled through the pages as he turned them. And he looked like he did not know Llub was standing next to him until a shift in the wind crossed through the tent.

"Ah, you are the Itor on the journey," softly breathed the Pedisax, "I am Omter of the Pedisax from the Tribe Vomryo. Our tribe is a master of this world, as wild as it may seem. It has been many generations since we have encountered someone or a group speaking of an enemy to harm, invade, and kill us all. The Kernanites must be stopped. You know this for a fact. I feel your pain. Your ancestors speak here. You almost lost your homeworld and your species entirely."

"What's your secret?" Llub said in an untrustworthy tone of voice.

"I have no secret. I am here to see our younger ones off to see their great ancestors so they may ascend through the Tribe, as you can see."

Omter looked with pleasure at the other Pedisax. He pulled at a thin beard. Then, he looked at Llub again.

"All the species and races of this galaxy have something in common despite our fighting. Even then, the Pedisax remember a time of great peace throughout the galaxy. We remember a time of great trade and growth, but that only brought shame to the Pedisax. So, we retreated. Finally, taking refuge here in this unknown world, the Pedisax call Y'Fert. We weren't the first and hopefully not the last to inhabit Y'Fert," counseled Omert wisely.

"I've come to bargain with you, Omert," said Llub nervously. I wish to undergo one of your ascension rituals; maybe it will help my tribe fight the Kernanites."

"We do not like outsiders trying out sacred rituals." Omert looked up quizzically and then over to the fire as the Pedisax regained consciousness. He jammed his staff into the ground while uttering some solemn words from the book. In front of him, the Pedisax regained complete consciousness and stood up on their feet.

"Why exactly did you come before the Pedisax?" quipped Omert, "Who are you protecting?"

Llub thought for a while in front of Omert. The Pedisax had been following *him*. It was not the reverse. Atticus and the group had kept to themselves, especially since Aida's child was born. They were undoubtedly protecting Sicro and holding Captain Reno prisoner until he could be trusted. *How will the child grow up in this galaxy?* He was Atticus's closest confidant, if not the only person he was around for the longest time besides Aida. Llub knew he trusted him. Llub's need for comfort, survival of his species, and protection of the child won over, and he chose to reveal they were protecting an unborn child.

"We are protecting someone, and we have someone held as a prisoner. Unfortunately, the prisoner is a friend we need," said Llub.

"An unborn child? And, how will this child grow up?" said Omert. He touched a signet on the book, and it began to glisten and glow. Omert began to speak the Pedisax language.

"I am asking our ancestors Llub for an answer," sang Omert.

When the song ended, Omert looked very peaceful. He closed the book and stood on his six legs. He showed some pride and sadness.

"The child is a refugee. He is…unique. A Humar is an ancient race related to the Kernanites, which no one knew until recently. He's also a restorer. His father is from the planet of D'Er and Stie Lux—planets of royalty, civility, and honor," said the Pedisax enthusiastically.

"How do you know this?" Llub questioned.

Omert laughed.

"My ancestors knew him before he was born. And, now the Pedisax knows. I saw him before Nomop, the god of the Pedisax. If he is the restorer to Atticus's royal house and Atticus loves Aida, we will win the war with the Kernanites," said Omert. He clapped his hands and looked more joyful than usual for someone coming from a trance.

"What do you know of the future of my homeworld?" said Llub.

"The Kernanites are now a great scourge to your people," said Omert to Llub.

"Is there hope? A solution at all?" said Llub.

"There is only hope, love, and faith now," said Omert.

Llub quickly realized he needed to get back to camp where Atticus and the group were. He took some seeds from the Pedisax, which looked like they would help their farming cause. As he exited Omert's tent, he thanked him graciously. The mighty winds of Y'Ert whipped against his clothes and face.

While Llub was gone, Atticus tended to Aida. Sweat formed into watery beads on her forehead. She breathed heavily and grabbed whatever she could find. She was beginning to give birth. Atticus wondered if Llub would arrive to see the birth of the child.

"What will we name the child?" said Atticus.

"Sicro—if it's a boy—and Vey if it's a girl," said Aida.

Llub appeared at the tent's entrance with some of the seeds given to him by the Pedisax. He looked over at Aida. He smiled.

"I almost thought I had missed it," said Llub.

"She is about halfway through the Humarian birthing process," said Atticus.

"The Pedisax know about the child," said Atticus.

Atticus raised an eyebrow. He clapped his hands on Llub's shoulder. And, he laughed.

"Everyone can know about this birth. It is not in Aida's custom nor mine to keep it a secret," said Atticus.

Llub and Atticus knelt beside Aida. She pushed and pushed until the baby could be seen covered in blue Humarian blood. In a couple of seconds, they heard the cry of the newborn.

"Is it a boy or girl?" said Aida.

"It's a boy," said Atticus.

"So, it's Sicro then," said Aida.

"Yes, it's Sicro," agreed Atticus.

Sciro was born amid the harsh winds of Y'Fert. His name meant *refuge* in Aida's native tongue. At the time of Sicro's birth, Aida and Atticus were twenty-five years old in Stie Luxian years.

Fourteen years passed, and Sicro grew into a tall and strong teenager. The group still lived on Y'Fert. Sicro had not seen much besides the world of Y'Fert, but there was much to explore on his homeworld. Growing up, he played with some Pedisax.

For Sicro's education, there was the sage of the Pedisax Tribe nearby. Omert had passed away about two years after Sicro was born, so a new Pedisax ascended to Omert's rank. When a new Pedisax ascended to Omert's title of sage, he took lessons from him. The sage's name was Oywort.

Sicro had more than once heard the story of his parent's journey to the Independent Worlds, Ba'Gam, and all the worlds they encountered. One day, Sicro skipped rocks on a pond by the river when his father approached him.

"When was the last time you have seen Reno?" said Atticus.

"The last time I saw him, he was by the irrigation canals," said Sicro.

Atticus sighed. He needed to speak to Reno soon but did not want Sicro to know why all communications to and from the Independent Worlds had gone dark. Atticus saw something different in Sicro—like he knew something more after all these days and years on Y'Fert.

Atticus needed to find the Pedisax. They are always up for a gamble. He needed to ensure Sicro did not know the Independent Worlds were the truth. *They halfway brought up the boy and into a young man.* They should know what to do. Atticus followed the river and left Sicro for his own business. *Who will the boy grow into be in this now harsh galaxy?* Atticus gently massaged his head to try to forget these perplexing thoughts.

As Atticus walked along the riverside, he found a main Pedisax camp of the local Tribe they had been conversing with all these years. He saw smoke billowing out of the tent. He saw a few Pedisax putting water into jugs by the river. Atticus wandered to the main tent and stepped into it. To his surprise, Aida was there. She looked sad. Atticus could not think of what could bother her, but her emotion was unusual after all these years.

"You won't be here," she said. Aida held back tears in her eyes. "It will be for the best, though. For all."

Atticus did not understand what she said, and he did not like the sound. She threw more dust the Pedisax had given her into a fire in the middle of the tent. Atticus just stood there. The sage beckoned for him to move over to his side of the fire.

"You are on the right side, my son," said the old Pedisax sage.

Atticus gently sat beside him, and the sage patted his back. The sage looked happy and then looked over at Aida. Some of his servants came to his side and gave him some cold water.

"On this harsh world, we share," said the sage. He took some of his water and filled it in two other cups. He gave them to Aida and Atticus.

Aida looked happier at the gesture. Atticus was more relaxed. The sage coughed.

"The two that were met, joined, and underwent a journey," said the sage. "A journey yet to be completed."

Aida's eyes lit, and Atticus saw something he had not seen since they first escaped the Kernanites. A swirl of blue energy enveloped Aida. And, the sage began to chant. At first, Atticus did not recognize the tone or style of his words when he sang louder, but it was a prayer he was saying.

Soon, the swirl enveloped Atticus as well. Immediately, his mind was filled with images of Sicro. He did not see his future. He saw the past here on Y'Fert.

He saw his son joined to his mother, his birth, and his growing years. Then he saw fire. That is all Atticus saw while the swirl of blue energy enveloped him. His old tattoo on his arm began to glow. It signaled an enemy was near Atticus, the group, the Pedisax, and Y'Fert. But who and where is the enemy coming from? Atticus thought about the blackout from the Independent Worlds.

While they were on Y'Fert, the Independent Worlds had reported safe, and so had most of the galaxy. The Kernanites had stopped their invasions and pillaging for an unknown reason. This meeting with the sage provided no new knowledge about their movements. Atticus still felt that it was his duty, first and foremost, to protect Stie Lux and the other Independent Worlds. While they had stayed on Y'Fert, Atticus thought they might even make the long journey to D'Er.

When the swirl of blue energy disappeared, Atticus gasped and found three Pedisax looking over him. The sage seemed almost finished praying, and the Pedisax servants tended to him. Atticus knew he had to tell Sicro the truth, and the day seemed closer after what had just happened.

Aida looked content. Better than when Atticus entered the tent. Atticus' tattoo slowly stopped glowing, and the blue energy faded from Aida. The sage beckoned to his servants to help him to stand on his old legs.

"I must see your child Aida and Atticus," said the sage.

Atticus held up his hand. He had always trusted the Pedisax with Sicro. He felt the difference in the air. The Pedisax had something in store for Sicro, him, and the group.

When they approached Sicro, he was with Captain Reno. The sage brought five of his servants, and once he saw Reno, he hesitated. After a time, the sage pointed.

"This man has nefarious intent," said the sage.

Atticus gently smiled and took to Sicro's side. He motioned to Aida to stand with them. Looking at Reno, he addressed the sage.

"His infamous tendencies have been corrected. He was a soldier and warrior from the Star Union who provided help at the beginning of our journey and still does," said Atticus.

The sage looked around at the farm and irrigation canals Reno tended to with approval. He still eyed Reno, and while he did, he brought out a bag holding the dust the Pedisax use for their prayer sessions and trances around fires. Holding the dust in his hand, he threw it in the canal and onto the vegetables on the farm.

Immediately, the water became more apparent, and the vegetables looked cleaner and grew slightly. Llub saw all the activity and walked from the group's main encampment area. Once he saw Llub, the sage stepped back and looked him up and down with weary eyes.

"This—this Itor knows our sacred rituals," said the sage.

Atticus lifted an eyebrow. He was not aware Llub had consorted with them recently. Llub straightened up and looked at the sage.

"It was long ago," said Llub.

The sage looked satisfied at the response and became formal. The servants presented Atticus and the groups with more bags.

"Then, we will trade," said the Pedisax sage.

XIII

It was an unusually cloudy day on Y'Fert. It was even more unusual to hear the low rumble throughout the plain. The Pedisax had grown closer to Atticus, Sicro, Aida, and the group. Captain Reno and Sicro used some old manuals given to them by the Pedisax to help them farm. In the main tent, Atticus stayed attentive to the communication console on the Star Jumper. The blackout from the Independent Worlds continued. In fact, on some days, it wasn't easy to transmit a message to and from Y'Fert.

Aida stood atop a dune, listening to the wind skirt around her body. She moved her scarf and headgear against her crystal skin. The sound of the wind was almost musical as she listened on top of the dune and looked out onto the plain below and the river. Atticus found Adia, and he quietly moved up from behind her, not wanting to scare her. The sound of *hodit* roaming the plain was also heard.

Atticus stood beside Aida, grabbed her shoulder, and hugged her. It had been hard to get into intimacy lately.

"Remember on Fina when we first met?" said Atticus. "I thought your skin was beautiful." Her green eyes turned bright with his comforting words.

Aida, though, turned abruptly away from him. She crossed her arms and moved down the dune. Then, she turned to Atticus.

"I told Sicro the secret. Everything. I told him you were born in Stie Lux, and your mother and father were from D'Er and Stie Lux. He did not believe me. He did not want to believe me that we kept running. Who would? He said he would have stayed and fought. I told him he had forgotten that I was the one who had fallen in love with a royal who was on Fina. The reason why we kept running was for the sake of the Independent Worlds and the galaxy," said Aida to Atticus.

Atticus was stunned. They had built their lives on Y'Fert for many years without these topics and secrets brought into conversation. *Why now?* Atticus thought.

"I feel like there is more work here on Y'Fert," said Aida. "We're not ready to pick up and resume our journey like the Pedisax said during their prayer session."

"Have you ever thought it was *just* a prayer with no meaning? They still do not like outsiders, so why would you trust them?" said Atticus.

"I trust them because it is what is left. Ba'Gam and the Kernanites are on the move. I sense it. The Independent Worlds have not reestablished contact," said Aida angrily.

"We know nothing about what is going on right now, and what happened in the past is in the past. Stop carrying it with you," consoled Atticus.

"And you as well," said Aida with a glare.

"Captain Reno thinks he can strengthen the communications array on the Star Jumper. On a side note, he's doing better. He has learned the fault in his decisions," said Atticus.

Aida stared directly into Atticus's eyes. Atticus stared back, first in loving warmth and then with resolve. *She is challenging him*, he thought. *But with what?*

Atticus continued to look over the plain and river with Aida. He prayed for an answer to know who or what was bothering her. The *hodit* continued to roam about the plain and grunt noisily.

In the distance, they saw two forms form into two distinct figures. It was Captain Reno and Llub. The prayer was answered. Aida threw down her scarf and huffed.

"Where's Sicro?" said Atticus.

"We left him at camp," said Reno.

Atticus scowled, and Aida crossed her arms. Llub and Captain Reno saw the negative emotions but continued pursuing them. Llub had a star map with him.

"Ba' Gam and the Kernanite Alliance are on the move again. They have invaded here and here. They were trade worlds, but worlds with their history, art, and culture," said Llub somberly.

Aida's back stiffened, and she abruptly looked at Atticus. Her green eyes grew even fiercer. Atticus knew the words coming next were about Sicro.

"Sicro now needs to know. He needs to know everything. And I mean everything that led us to Y'Fert. Your services are now in need, Reno. Can you train Sicro to fight? Your treason is forgiven if you train him," said Atticus.

"When will the Kernanites and Ba'Gam get here?" said Aida.

"In about a month or two. Luckily, I got the communications array working again on the Star Jumper. I found they were jamming the signal between the Independent Worlds and us. The Independent Worlds are safe, but not for very much longer. I sent a communication to them, and it looks like I am expecting one in return," said Reno.

The day quickly turned into twilight as the group of four headed back to camp. Aida looked up at the sky as the galaxy of stars blazed in front of her. Atticus held her hand. They said goodnight to Llub and Reno, and they parted ways. They crossed by Sicro's tent, and he was already asleep. Yesterday will be a new day on their journey to freedom.

The days passed slowly since they got word that Ba'Gam and the Kernanite Alliance were on the move. Llub took Reno's place, fixing the Star Jumper and monitoring communications. Aida and Atticus took to handling the farm.

Atticus and Aida were on the farm when they suddenly heard the Star Jumper whiz into the air. Atticus held his arm in front of his face because the dust was kicked up into the air. Aida turned her back and looked at a monitor on her belt.

"It looks like Sicro has learned how to fly a Star Jumper," said Aida.

"Only from the best," said Atticus.

The Star Jumper flew low, and Sicro waved at his parents. He buckled in tightly and plugged in coordinates, and the Star Jumper fully came to life.

"Where to?" said Sicro.

Sicro took the Star Jumper on short excursions many times. He liked the openness of the space around Y'Fert—nothing harmful. Despite his freedom, he constantly communicated with Llub through a small communicator back on the surface.

"How's the view?" said Llub to Sicro through the communicator.

"It's great! I can almost see the main continent from here! It's beautiful!" said Sicro.

Sicro had been watching a spot against the blackness of space grow bigger and smaller. It grew so big that it almost seemed like a new star had been born, but Sicro knew somehow it was not.

"I'm going to go further to check something out in the distance," said Sicro.

"There's nothing out there, but be safe!" said Llub.

As soon as Sicro got the Star Jumper in the direction of the spot, it grew larger and brighter. The cockpit was filled with light, and the Star Jumper was consumed by it. Sicor let out a scream.

"What is it?" said Llub.

"I—I don't know—I can't see anything—but the Star Jumper seems OK. There is light everywhere," said Sicro.

Llub was on the planet's surface, checking the readings for any foreign activity in the space around Y'Fert. There was a spike in the readings, so Llub grabbed the communicator.

"Get out of there!" said Llub to Sicro.

Sicro got out of his pilot's chair and quickly looked at the readings on the science and communications consoles. The Kernanite Alliance had arrived. A vast number of warships had just dropped out of hyperspace. The Star Jumper started to shake, and Sicro looked out one of the windows of the Star Jumper. Massive warships—the largest man-made things he had ever seen—slowly moved past the Star Jumper.

"Llub," said Sicro with his voice shaking. "They're here."

"Who's they?" said Llub to Sicro.

Llub looked up at the sky. The question was answered. Massive warships were now locking themselves into orbit around Y'Fert.

"Don't come back home just yet, Sicro, until we find out what is going on," said Llub.

Llub moved from where he stood on top of a dune and walked to the farm. Captain Reno was running in his direction. He was loading his gun.

Llub held his hand up to Reno to calm him down and prevent him from loading even more shots into his gun. Reno looked frightened about the orbiting warships. Llub moved Reno aside and went to look for Aida and Atticus.

"We need to move with the Pedisax," said Reno. "They have caves to hide in further into the desert."

Standing atop the dune, Llub continued searching for Aida and Atticus. In the distance, he saw two *hodit* riders from the Pedisax. Llub squinted against the harsh sun of Y'Fert. The forms of riders got closer, and then Llub yelled. It was Aida and Atticus.

"Where's Sicro?" panted Atticus.

Llub gave him a look of disappointment and sadness. Llub knew he was safe. *He'll come back*, thought Llub.

"He's in the Star Jumper orbiting around Y'Fert," said Llub.

"Wait—What?" said Aida.

"We were doing our daily spin with the Star Jumper, and then suddenly, the Kernanite Alliance came," said Llub.

"How do you know it's them?" said Atticus.

Atticus looked up through the clouds. *They were warships, alright. But from where?*

Atticus grabbed an optic viewer to look at the warships. Suddenly, one big, massive one came out of nowhere to the right of Atticus' vision. It had the emblem of the Kernanite Alliance. A white star superimposed on a circular blue background.

"We have to get to the Pedisax caves," said Llub.

"I am not leaving without Sicro," said Atticus.

"I'll go with you," said Aida.

Captain Reno was packing a *hodit* with more goods and pieces of technology. He waived over to Llub to come over to assist him. Llub walked over and grabbed a map from Reno's hands.

"The caves are north of the dunes," said Reno.

Llub looked over as to what Reno was bringing. He saw Aida's box with her tiara in it. *Could Captain Reno be trusted again?* thought Llub. Everyone will have to find out the hard way.

"Go with the Pedisax to the caves. I will help Aida and Atticus bring Sicro back," said Llub.

As soon as he said that, he could hear the sound of explosions. The Pedisax and the caves were under attack already. He looked back at the encampment. The Kernanites had not spotted it yet. He could see Aida and Atticus going over to the tent, but then Llub realized he had something they needed. The teleporter was on his utility belt! He began running to the encampment in hopes the Alliance would not find it first.

Llub was out of breath by the time he got to the encampment. The harsh winds of Y'Fert moved through the tents. All three of them covered their faces with scarves.

"I have the teleporter," said Llub.

"Good, we need it! We'll teleport Sicro back from the Star Jumper. He can put it on autopilot," said Atticus.

Aida's eyes darted back with concern from Atticus to Llub. She did not like the sound of it. *The Alliance may capture him,* she thought.

"If we are going to do something, we need to do it now," said Aida.

"Llub set up the teleporter, and I'll communicate to Sicro that we are ready," said Atticus.

Aida looked up at the sky. The clouds were soon parting to let the yellow hue of the sky through. She looked over at Llub.

From nowhere, they heard the bang and boom of several explosions and what seemed like planes moving through the sky. Aida and Atticus walked out of a tent. Some passing Pedisax were pointing at the sky.

"Those are Alliance starship fighters," said Atticus.

"Atticus! We must teleport Sicro now," said Aida.

"I'm on it," said Atticus, "Atticus to Sicro. Get into the teleport position in twenty seconds."

As Sicro got ready for teleportation, he saw the starship fighters swirl around Y'Fert. He felt the tingling sensation of the teleportation undulate through his body. His last glimpse was of the starship fighters suddenly bombarding the planet.

"Sicro, over here," said Atticus.

The bombardment by the starship fighters had begun on Y'Fert. Sicro got onto a *hodit* and hurriedly went towards the caves. Llub and Reno followed him. Aida and Atticus were in the front. Fusion torpedoes lit up the sky as the *hodit* galloped with their riders to the protection of the caves.

When they were almost to the caves, some Pedisax surrounded the group of five with whirlwind shields. The shields formed a dome barrier for the group to maneuver and get protection from the torpedoes. It was only a short while until the group reached the caves.

Once in the caves, the *hodit* galloped into the protection of waiting stalls. The *hodit* was exhausted, and so was everyone else. The caves shook, and dirt fell from the ceiling as more fusion torpedoes pounded the area.

Atticus leaped down from his ride and walked to the location of a warrior chief of the Pedisax. The Pedisax was from the local tribe Atticus, and the others often communicated with daily. He blew the hodit horn whenever Pedisax or strangers entered the caves for safety.

"Where is the sage from the Tribe Vomryo?" said Atticus.

A warrior Pedisax grunted. He opened up a location finder with one of his six crab-like legs. The locator beeped, and the warrior Pedisax grunted again.

"He's further down in the cave system surrounded by guards," said the warrior, "My assistant Ret will take you to him."

"Thank you," said Atticus. He ran to the group to find Aida, who was unpacking when he saw her.

"I'm taking Sicro to see the sage," said Atticus.

"Yes, that is a good idea. We do not have much time before the fighting starts," said Aida.

Aida waved over to Sicro, who was unpacking from his hodit. His youthful look blazed like hope in darkness amidst the attack. Sicro was *hope*.

Sicro and Atticus began exploring the cavern system. Eventually, they found the sage's cave, which contained numerous attendants and Pedisax warriors.

Once the sage saw Atticus and Sicro, he began to pray in a song. The attendants splashed some of the dust for prayer into a jug holding a fire. Once the sage finished praying, he stood straight up, snorted, and drank the dust from the jug.

"The Pedisax have seen a vision. A time of great conflict is upon all of us. The boy named Sicro deserves our protection," said the sage.

Sicro looked down at the cave floor. He did not know what to say. Atticus patted his son on the shoulder. He knew Sicro would bring about the journey again, but he did not realize it until recently.

XIV

Dust fell from the cavern ceilings as more bombing runs from the starship fighters of the Kernanite Alliance took place. Sicro clutched his fists as his father looked at him. Atticus tended to use the heater to keep the cave warm during those cold nights.

Aida was in the corner making some soup with some rations. Llub monitored the sensors, which could pick up ground or aerial movement around the caves. Outside the inner cave where Llub, Aida, Atticus, and Sicro were, Captain Reno paced back and forth. He continually monitored the communications technology on his belt. He remained quiet most of the time while they sought refuge in the cave.

The bombardment continued for weeks. The Pedisax never gave way in their fight to the Kernanite Alliance. Atticus and the others felt pride about it all, but it had been hard. Day after day, crouching in a cave tired the group of five.

One morning, Atticus woke up to see some Pedisax crushed by the boulders that had fallen from the cavern. Atticus brought over Sicro and the others. They were frightened, but a Pedisax chief sang a prayer and said brave words in a speech.

Sicro was sleeping beside Atticus one night when he tapped Atticus on the shoulder. Atticus did not want to turn over and speak to Sicro, but his fatherly instincts won over this time. He turned.

"Father, when will we meet the enemy?" said Sicro.

Atticus impatiently sighed. "You never want to meet the enemy; you only want to out-strategize them."

Sicro pondered this unsatisfactorily. He kept his utility belt close and his ion gun in case the Alliance broke through their defenses. They all slept soundly with the gentle hum of light generators heard in the cave.

A loud bang was heard. Sicro jumped from his sleep. Atticus was right beside him. Captain Reno drew his ion gun, and so did Llub. Aida hid in the corner of the cave. The Pedisax in the cavern next to theirs began firing their weapons. Some were hit. Shouting and yelling were heard throughout the caves.

"Stay here, everyone," said Atticus, "I'll go to the roof of the caves and catch them from the top."

Atticus found the stair-like passageway to the roof of the caverns, and once he reached it, he looked down on the fighting below him. To his left were five or six Kernanite Alliance warriors. They were called the Hynox. To the right was the Pedisax, taking cover behind boulders and pillars inside the caverns.

A high-energy ion shot glanced past him from a Hynox. They began to point. Atticus grabbed his ion weapon and laid belly down on the cavern floor. He raised himself gently and found a Hynox directly in his sight. He shot at him several times, and the Hynox was hit. Luckily, he did not have any shielding on at the time.

Sweat poured down Atticus' forehead and shirt. He sat back on the cavern wall. He wanted to shoot at them more, but he needed cover from the Pedisax. He grabbed his utility belt and inputted a message to them.

More Hynox warriors spilled into the caves. Their weapons were drawn, and a few threw ion grenades at the Pedisax. Beneath Atticus, the Pedisax continually came up and fired one of their most formidable weapons, which is translated in Atticus' language as the *slicer*. It fires ion bursts after bursting through enemy lines. Three to six Hynox warriors fell. The Hynox waved their hands, beckoning more warriors to enter the cave. The *slicer* continued its assault on them until all the Hynox held their fists in the air and did not waiver even though they were being shot at and falling dead.

Suddenly, loud thuds were heard, and in the dust of the mayhem. Gigantic, eerily made robots that created a suit for Hynox warrior appeared. When several entered the cave, the suited Hynox unleashed their firepower. Atticus oversaw all this and took some of the Hynox out with his ion gun. He felt a tap on his shoulder.

It was Sicro. He looked frightened and bewildered. Atticus knew what it was about as a father.

"It's time, Sicro. Don't freeze up now. It's time to use what you learned in training with Reno, Llub, and I," said Atticus to his son.

"I'm scared, Dad," said Sicro.

"As soon as you take out a couple of those warriors, you'll be experiencing the thrill of your life," said Atticus.

Yells and cheers were heard from the Pedisax. Atticus looked down at the battle. Several Hynox were taken out in the fighting. The Pedisax *slicer* was still working effectively. Atticus touched his utility belt to summon Llub and Reno. Atticus looked at his son, and he saw a glow reflected in his eyes. It was his tattoo. The enemy— Ba'Gam of the Kernanite Alliance was near. Llub and Captain Reno positioned themselves on the cave's opposite side, looking down at the fighting.

Atticus gave them a cue, and they began to fire at will. Sicro crotched down on his belly next to his father. He sensed his father was not at all nervous. So, Sicro puffed himself up and began firing at the Hynox.

"Great job, Sicro," said Atticus.

Sicro let out a laugh and a whoop as several Hynox fell before him. The Hynox began to notice the firing from above them. They threw up some ion grenades, but a Pedisax shield stopped them. There was a lull in the fighting. The Pedisax became relaxed but then became agitated. One of their warriors had a *hodit* horn on him and blew through the horn. He now was warning the other Pedisax of more enemies on the move.

Dark shadows were cast into the cave as Hynox in suits filled the opening. They formed a line, then a column, and began to part, letting in a figure. On the other side of the cavern from Atticus, Llub noted the new figure. He used his Itorian-enhanced senses to determine who was approaching them. It was Ba'Gam.

"Llub to Atticus," said Llub, "I have confirmation Ba'Gam is here."

Ba'Gam was wearing one of the war suits the Hynox was wearing. His colossal form cradled inside the metallic suit. The Pedisax regrouped around some of their positions. Fairly soon, Ba'Gam stood alone in the opening of the cave.

"Atticus, if you can hear me, I am finally here. You know you have always wanted to kill me, and now is your chance, and the feeling is likewise," said Ba'Gam.

Atticus and Sicro were still on their stomach. The feeling of wanting to shield Sicro from seeing his nemesis filled his body. He knew he should not protect him. It was time, after all, for Sicro to show Atticus what he was on Y'Fert.

Ba'Gam waved his suit hands and arms open in a gesture of openness. Atticus squinted. He could barely take the lie. Ba'Gam knew Atticus was there to kill him. *Why the necessities?* Atticus thought.

"It is all about where you are headed now, Atticus. I have been tracking and watching you. You have always eluded me. But…now…I have you right where I want you…and hopefully dead by the end of this battle," said Ba'Gam.

After briefly looking around him and telling Sicro to stay put, Atticus jumped down onto the cavern floor below. Ba'Gam immediately looked at him. He smirked.

"That's cute, you know…Your magical symbol is detecting me," said Ba'Gam to Atticus.

"It's my ancestral tattoo," said Atticus, "It's meant to detect your race…your species, if you will."

"Well, Kernanites and your type, Atticus, are not that different. We are almost cousins. We are almost family," said Ba'Gam.

Atticus smirked back at Ba'Gam. He clenched his fists as blue energy surged down his arms into a ball in his hands. Ba'Gam pounded the cavern floor with the metal arms of the suit. Hynox warriors swarmed around Ba'Gam. Atticus took the first shot. He killed some of the Hynox soldiers before Ba'Gam could move on him.

Energy pulses from the *slicers* of the Pedisax whirled past Atticus. He could tell shots were being fired by Captain Reno and Llub. Ba'Gam powered up his energy weapon and fired it straight at Atticus. Atticus blocked it with an energy shield as he crossed his arms and held them up high.

Grinding his teeth, Atticus jettisoned the energy pulse back at Ba'Gam, reeling him to the floor. The Pedisax let out a yell and a whoop, but they were still Hynox warrior to deal with, and Ba'Gam would soon get back up and fight some more.

Suddenly, more blue energy came from behind Atticus. Atticus turned and looked behind him. It was Aida. She was fully glowing in her Humarian blue energy.

"You want my son and me," said Aida. You will have to get me first."

Ba'Gam was entirely up as Aida approached, and when she threw her blue energy at him, he blocked it with a shield. He smirked and waved at more Hynox soldiers to come into the cave. Atticus drew an energy shield around him and Aida.

"It seems we are evenly matched, Atticus and Aida," said Ba'Gam, "The heir to the D'Er royal house and his Humarian love. What exactly are you trying to do? I once thought I could live in peace and prosperity until a Humarian warship came to a Kernanite colony and murdered my family. They were tortured, experimented on, and held in prison. All because they were part of the Kernanite clan and pledged non-violence. You see, things have changed. We're violent now."

Atticus and Aida both held the blue energy in their hands while Ba'Gam spoke. As he continued talking, Llub and Captain Reno crept down from the uppermost part of the cavern to the lines of Pedisax.

"So, take your best shot, Atticus and Aida. Then, I'll do it for you. All in fair game," said Ba'Gam.

Suddenly, Atticus heard footsteps behind him, and Sicro appeared out of the corner of his eye. Sicro was calm, with an intense look in his eyes. Blue energy hovered over his body, and Sicro melded it into his hands.

"Sicro, get back," said Atticus.

"No, father," argued Sicro, "This guy is after me and everyone I have ever known and loved. It's time to take care of him the hard way."

Ba'Gam smiled big and wide at Sicro's statement and devotion to his people. He wanted more and felt they would give it to him. More Hynox warriors readied themselves; the same thing happened with the Pedisax.

"You're Sicro," said Ba'Gam, "I don't just want you. I want the galaxy to submit to my will; the Kernanite will forever."

"Do you think we will go quietly," said a voice. Ba'Gam looked around, and the Pedisax parted their lines. It was Llub.

"Ah, Llub, proud and strong until the end. An Itor for eternity, I see," said Ba'Gam.

Llub charged his ion gun, and his green eyes shimmered with might. He approached Ba'Gam diagonally and eventually made his way to Aida's side. He pointed the ion gun directly at Ba'Gam.

"You'll have to take me too. And the Star Union, for that matter," said Captain Reno.

Ba'Gam laughed and slammed his mechanical arms to the ground in hysteria. Some of the Hynox warriors chuckled as well. The Pedisax grimaced and readied their weapons, and so did everyone else.

"You and your son are the key. All of you are the key to Kernanite control of the galaxy. The Itors, the Star Union, the Humars, the Independent Worlds, and D'Er all will be gone after I kill you. And their memory will go along with you. It will be turned to nothing," said Ba'Gam.

Sicro looked around him and spotted an undetonated ion grenade. He threw it at Ba'Gam's face. It exploded, and immediately, the Hynox opened fire. The Pedisax returned their fire, killing many of the Hynox.

A large energy pulse was heard and seen. Everyone exchanged shots. Atticus began to yell, and Aida did too. Atticus felt something on his shirt. It was blood. The blood of Sicro was on him.

"No…no…no…no! Shouted Atticus.

"Atticus," yelled Aida, "take cover and move to Sicro."

"We're covering them, Aida!" said Captain Reno and Llub jointly.

All four of them were up against a cave wall, breathing heavily. Despite this, Atticus checks to see if Sicro is still alive. He was not, as he had no pulse. Atticus opened Sicro's utility belt for a medical scan, which confirmed that Sicro was no longer living.

Wailing aloud in mourning, he got up and charged at Ba'Gam. Atticus's whole body was on the left mechanical arm of Ba'Gam. An overcharged ion gun was jammed into the suit's arm.

"Aida, get down," said Atticus.

The ion gun exploded, spewing the fluid, keeping the suit working everywhere. Ba'Gam jumped and then rolled out from the suit. He had a small dagger and sent it flying into Aida's heel. She screamed in pain.

"You just took my son's life, Ba'Gam, so for that…I must kill you," said Atticus.

Aida crawled her way over to her son. She wailed aloud in the morning and then grew red with rage in the face. She grabbed her ion gun, which was now hanging on her utility, and sent more shots at Ba'Gam.

The Pedisax continued to cut down Hynox soldiers. Ba'Gam slammed his right mechanical arm onto Atticus. Luckily, Atticus' shield was protecting him. Atticus jumped down from Ba'Gam and his suit. He stepped back and felt for a Pedisax slicer that had fallen on the ground.

Atticus took the *slicer* and hit Ba'Gam's suit. The left side of Ba'Gam's suit was melted, gnarled, and punched with the power of the *slicer*. Ba'Gam jumped through an escape hatch from the back of the suit. Hynox warriors gathered around him.

"I'll kill you one day, Atticus, and take the rest of the galaxy with me," said Ba'Gam. The Hynox warriors and Ba'Gam move away from the Pedisax line of fighting. They gradually faded into an approaching dust storm.

Atticus dropped to his knees. Exhausted, he stared at the cavern floor as dust swept in from outside the cave. Feeling his chest cave in, he let out a sob and a scream. He could hear some Pedisax warriors approaching from behind him.

"Atticus," said a Pedisax, "Your son is dead, but we have one over Y'Fert because the Kernanite Alliance is dropping out of orbit and retreating. You, Aida, and the rest are safe."

Atticus raised his head and used the staff on the *slicer* to help himself up from the cavern floor. His brown hair moved quickly through the wind. Aida was still heard crying. Llub and Captain Reno ran over to Atticus with looks of desperation. They all had lost their only hope on this journey.

XV

Atticus put more wood on the Sicro's funeral pyre. The fire blazed high into the night sky. Captain Reno knelt while saying prayers of the Pedisax. In the distance, Llub sharpened his sword on the river's banks, listening to whitewater crash against boulders. In a Pedisax make-shift tent, Aida tended to mix some herbs and spices with the ceremonial food.

"The Pedisax have suggested we offer some herbs and spices to the river gods," said Llub to Aida.

The funeral pyre crackled, spraying yellow and orange embers everywhere. Atticus quickly moved to stomp them out with his feet. Realizing he needed to send one final communication to Stie Lux before he ended his day and said some prayers next to the fire. The funeral pyre was dug into the ground to contain the fire. Occasionally, Llub looked at Reno. And Atticus wandered over to where Captain Reno was saying prayers. Aida joined them and threw some herbs and spices into the fire.

Sitting cross-legged, Aida cleared her throat and rubbed some tree ochre on her forehead and arms. Atticus noted a lone tear drop down her right cheek, and then she sobbed again. She buried her head in her hands.

Captain Reno stood up after saying his prayers and went over to Llub. The eerie screech from Llub's sword filled the air as Captain Reno reclined against a *hodit* tent. Some Pedisax let their youngsters play in the distance, so Reno decided to protect them.

With their many legs, the youngsters kicked a ball around in a field near the encampment. Reno looked up at a starry night sky with falling stars occasionally crossing the broad field of the sky. He wondered when the Kernanite Alliance would return. Recently, rumors of raiders allied to the Kernanites reached everyone. Atticus was still the one to make the strategies and movements if the enemy approached.

Llub continued to brandish his sword while listening to some classical Itorian music. The light, musical sounds coursed through the air of the desert night. The wind ruffled the tents of the encampment, and the funeral pyre slowly stopped burning. Atticus grabbed some hodit to cover the pyre with dirt thoroughly. He worked through the night, and the pyre was buried in the sand by morning.

Atticus tied some *hodit* to dead trees on the banks of the river. He brushed off some dirt from his shirt. Clunking and clinking of metal was heard from the Star Jumper. The Pedisax managed to camouflage the Star Jumper during the attack, saving it from destruction.

Taking a seat on the ramp to get into the Star Jumper, he pondered again what could happen next on Y'Fert. The cool spray from the river's whitewater drifted onto his face through the air. The smell of water in an arid environment was unique to Atticus. He got up and walked into the Star Jumper. Llub was sitting at the central command console. Atticus knew what he was up to as he passed the communications, science, and operations consoles. They were consuming large amounts of data and information.

"I'm recalibrating the Star Jumper, Atticus," said Llub.

"Indeed," said Atticus.

"The different arrays of the Star Jumper came out just fine through the fighting," said Llub.

Llub looked over at Atticus as he went to the back of the Star Jumper. Llub noticed Atticus was oddly holding himself—his chest sunken in with his shoulders out above his body. He was sobbing. Llub went over to Atticus and sat down near him.

"Sometimes we have to realize all the bad things in the galaxy happen for some reason. Things will pan out, Atticus. We are on a journey after all, and Sicro will be with us every step of the way," consoled Llub.

Standing up, Atticus wiped away some tears. *He needed to show strength for Aida and the group,* he thought. Atticus felt guilty that the others were on this journey. It was, after all, only his family who was once royal and was attacked by the Kernanites. The others were simply collateral damage. He would never tell either the group or Aida the opinion he held about the events which have happened on the journey.

Atticus walked to the doorway of the Star Jumper. The sunlight from outside cascaded onto the shadows cast by the bulkheads of the Star Jumper. He did not know what was in store for him, but he knew he had been strong enough to weather the hits the gods had given him.

He walked down the rampart of the Star Jumper onto the desert sands. To the right of the Star Jumper and about fifty feet away. Atticus could see Captain Reno hitting an old punching bag held by a dead tree. As Atticus walked over, some of the native birds cooed unceasingly. Atticus did not think much of the birds' sounds.

"Captain Reno!" he said, "It's a pleasure, as always, to see you back at our side in this struggle."

Reno politely stopped punching the bag. He looked up and spat into a bowl next to him. Sweat poured down from his face, and it looked like he had been using a mask to breathe in the dusty atmosphere of Y'Fert.

"Consider my recent actions on taking your side an apology after all these years," said Reno.

Giving Atticus a quizzical, he stood there before him. Reno lowered his hands to his side and unclenched them. He analyzed Atticus for a while. Reno could read the truth in his face. Trust was there.

"Do you think I've gone through all this punishing rehabilitation for nothing, Atticus?" said Reno.

"No, I don't," said Atticus.

"Then, why do I get the feeling you still do not believe I am completely on your side," said Reno.

"Well, maybe it's because you hail from the mighty Star Union, or you have a reputation now. I think it is both," said Atticus.

Reno just shook his head and spat into the bowl again. He clapped his dusty hands and ran his fingers through his dirty blonde hair. He found his captain's jacket and put it on over his shirt.

"Aida is going to make me some more clothes. I expect they will be the finest quality seen this side of the galaxy," said Reno to Atticus.

Atticus raised his hands. He wanted to indicate he did not mean to offend Reno. He still saw potential in his relationship with the group.

"Reno, you have earned your right to freedom. You could stay with us. You are welcome. The fates brought us together, so who is to say who will rip our relationship apart," said Atticus sincerely.

Slowly taking off his boxing gloves, Reno gave Atticus a perplexing look. He hit the punching bag without gloves hard. He stared at his hands for a while.

"I do not believe in the gods, Atticus, or fate," said Reno. "How I have gotten to where I am is solely with the help and work of these hands and body."

The dust of the desert swept through the encampment. The punching bag swung in the wind. Some *hodit* were heard in the distance, and the wind carried along the yells of the Pedisax corralling them.

In the distance, massive dust clouds rolled down the hills where the caverns were beneath the mountains. Suddenly, some of the *hodit* were heard roaring. The Pedisax started to send out their hoots and hollers. Someone was coming.

Atticus looked up towards the dust, hills, and mountains. He shielded the light of the twin suns from his eyes. The Pedisax *hodit* herders ran past him and Reno.

"Raiders!" shouted some of the Pedisax.

"They have come to try to finish us off in the name of the Kernanite Alliance. We'll win this battle, Atticus," said a young warrior of the Pedisax.

"To the Star Jumper, Reno," said Atticus, "I'll get Llub and Aida."

Llub was still brandishing his sword when he heard the rumbling of the raiders approaching them. Aida let out a scream, and she ran to the Star Jumper. Llub gathered what he could and ran to the Star Jumper as well. He waited outside until Atticus and Reno arrived.

"Thank you, Llub," said Atticus.

"Thanks again, friend," said Reno.

Atticus' communicator on his belt started to beep. It was one of the chiefs of the Pedisax. Atticus went over to the communication console.

"Atticus, we'll get them from the ground while you get them from the air. Is everyone safe?" said the chief.

"Yes, everyone is safe so far. I'm glad you have a strategy. We have enough weaponry to hold them off from the air," said Atticus.

Llub was at the pilot console, and Atticus sat beside him. They both could see the ion bursts fired from the raiders. The bursts were hitting what was left of the encampment and the farm. Once entirely in the air, Llub took the Star Jumper around the plain to face the on-coming raiders.

"What do they have in their arsenal, Reno?" said Atticus.

"They have some Yellow Bird fighters, some scout ships equipped with ion rays, and about five hundred infantries," said Reno.

"Not that bad of a fight," said Llub.

The Star Jumper suddenly shook violently, sparks coming from inside the ship's consoles. The raider scout ships zoomed past the Star Jumper, and Llub went after them.

"I have them in visual sight, Reno," said Llub.

"I have them, Llub. Opening fire," said Reno.

In an instant, two scouts exploded in the sky, and Reno and everyone yelled in relief. Llub took the Star Jumper for another shot at the raiders' forces in the air. Captain Reno scanned the surface to see the status of the Pedisax.

"The Pedisax are making their way through the defenses of the raiders, Atticus," said Reno.

"Atticus! This is Monto of the Pedisax," communicated a chief of the Pedisax via hologram. "We have the leader of the raiders in our hands. What do we do?"

"Hold him until we get rid of the raider forces in the air," said Atticus.

"Will do," said Monto.

"The last of the air forces is a Yellow Bird fighter, Atticus," said Llub.

"I'm locking onto him," said Reno.

Before Reno could open fire, the Yellow Bird fighter flipped in the air and went head-on toward the Star Jumper. The Yellow Bird opened fire, with some ion rays breaking through the Star Jumper shielding. Llub sped up the Star Jumper, and it staggered upwards past the Yellow Bird.

"I'm going to switch back everyone to catch the fighter from behind," said Llub.

The Star Jumper abruptly turned, and Captain Reno opened fire on the Yellow Bird fighter. The fighter was neutralized. From all the rapid movements, Atticus and everyone beside Llub looked blue in the face.

Aida slumped in her chair, trying to relax. It was over. Reno, too, fell back on a wall of the Star Jumper in exhaustion.

"I need to land the Star Jumper, Atticus," said Llub, "Where are the Pedisax? And, where are they holding the leader of the raiders?"

Atticus went to the console before him and looked at a map. The Star Jumper found the location of the Pedisax. They were near the edge of the river by the farm.

"Take us down by the farm, Llub," said Atticus.

The Star Jumper touched down on the dusty banks of the river. Aida and Reno put on some newer clothes. Llub and Atticus went outside and greeted the Pedisax chief, Monto. Atticus came up on a circle of the Pedisax where there was a hooded figure. The Pedisax whispered as to the fate of the leader. Atticus wanted to see him first.

Atticus knelt beside the leader and took off his hood. Everyone let out a gasp of shock. This was no typical raider plundering through the galaxy. The leader was a Stie Luxian.

"You're---You're—Stie Luxian," said Atticus.

Atticus analyzed the stranger's body. The tattooing was Stie Luxian. And, he was humanoid.

The Raider leader spat on the ground next to Atticus with a furrowed brow. He ground and clenched his teeth, trying to free himself of his manacles. Every time he moved too much, the manacles sent ions burst through him.

"Did you expect anything less, brother?" said the Raider leader.

Atticus took a step back while kneeling. He could not believe what he was hearing. *After everything that has happened, he finally met his family again*, he thought. The glare of the man calling himself Atticus's brother tore through Atticus's body. His mother and father never mentioned that he had a brother. The images of screams of people in the devastated cities by the Alliance on his homeworld flashed before his eyes. He tried to remember—anything—that would shed light on this new foe who was now kneeling right before him.

"Do you know this man, Atticus," said Monto.

"I don't—I don't know," said Atticus, "My mother and father—my family—never mentioned I had any siblings."

Monto read Atticus sincerely and the strange foe. He huffed and clicked his many legs through the sand. A few more raiders were brought to Atticus. Some of them were of races and species Atticus had never heard of, even in his travels. Raiders still, nonetheless.

"Take him, Monto, and put him in the caverns," said Atticus. "I'll decide what to do with him."

As soon as he said this, his tattoo started to glow, and the Stie Luxian raider looked back and yelled at Atticus. Both of their tattoos were glowing now. Running up to the Pedisax and the stranger, he wanted to ask the Stie Luxian again if he had any information.

"Do you know about Ba'Gam and the Alliance," said Atticus.

"You and I have the same enemy," said the raider.

"What's your name?" said Atticus.

"Pito is the name," said the raider.

Atticus looked at his tattoo again. It had the same glow as his. *Did the glowing mean the same thing?* He thought.

"I offer you some hope after the death of your son—or, as we should say now, my former nephew," said Pito.

Atticus grabbed his ion gun, wielded it, and pointed it at his head. Pito did not even budge.

"You know nothing about how my son died or him or what brought us here. So watch what you say. And, if you know anything and are keeping it from us, I will beat it out of you," said Atticus.

"I would rather go with your crab friends, brother," said Pito.

"Then, you better hope you haven't dashed your hopes and not mine," said Atticus.

The roaring of the river quickly drowned out the raiders' yells protesting their capture. The sunlight of the twin suns gradually changed to twilight. Atticus returned to the Star Jumper to camp and ward off the cold, desert night.

XVI

The cavern walls echoed Pito's screams. The whip cracked his back, and he gripped the cloth given to him. The Pedisax torturer grunted and grabbed Pito's head. The torturer arched Pito's back and threw him against the wall. Atticus was in the shadows, tossing a rock between his hands. Some blood spewed from Pito's mouth. Continuing to stare at Pito, Atticus then picked him up by his shackles.

"What do you know?" said Atticus.

"I know enough to put you in a grave!" said Pito.

Atticus punched his stomach. Pito gasped, and then he vomited. Pito's face plummeted onto the floor. Grabbing the back of Pito's neck, Atticus began to choke him.

"Tell me everything you know, or I'll kill you right here, right now," said Atticus.

Pito started to breathe heavily. He stared and stared at Atticus. Blood trickled from his mouth.

"Fine," said Pito, "Coordinates of where you were were given by me to Ba'Gam. Ba'Gam brought himself here. We're just raiders, Atticus. He did not know I was your long-lost brother, or he would have killed me. I guess," said Pito.

"You guess. You have pretty good diplomatic skills and are more cunning than average to pull that off," Atticus said.

Pito smiled a bloody smile. Laughter followed. He began to shake his hands and move his wrists.

"It was my nanny who was all the inspiration throughout my life. I never even got my own adopted mother and father. I heard about who I am and where I originate—from a sportsman I once met," said Pito.

"Oh, what sport," inquired Atticus.

"Tou-yo," said Pito, "You know, the one where you bounce balls off the wall and catch it with a gravity glove."

"That's a colonizer game, for starters. To inform of its history," said Atticus.

Pito cringed.

"Are you part of the secret Atticus?" said Pito, "You know the strange things about you and I. Why does our skin glow when pierced or near an adversary? I can see your tattoo glowing a little. Do you see me as an adversary? Don't you?"

Atticus did not have time for this small talk or pleasantries. Now that he knew Pito had confessed, he could move to other things. Pito looked tired and scared.

"Release him," said Atticus to a Pedisax soldier.

"Release him? But he's our only informant about the Alliance. I'll inform Chief Monto of this at once," said the soldier

"If he is truly my brother, more things will go in our favor," said Atticus.

The shackles came off from Pito. He immediately stood up and pushed Atticus. Pito was too quick. He landed a punch at Atticus' lower right jawline.

The Pedisax put a *slicer* to Pito's throat, causing him to stop. Atticus got up from the floor and took a step back from Pito. He looked at him steadily.

"You know, the soldier could lop off your head at any moment," said Atticus.

Pito's nostrils flared. He clenched his fists and rubbed his knuckles. Closing his eyes, he began to hum.

"You lied, Atticus," said Pito.

"About what?" said Atticus.

"Everything. The war, the Alliance, Fina. You lied to everyone to make it out of harm's way. Coward!" said Pito.

The Pedisax soldiers were alarmed by Pito and Atticus's display of anger. Atticus signaled to the Pedisax to let Pito loose with more guards. Three guards came into the cave, where they were all standing.

"One last thing Pito. I never really knew our parents either. You have a good punch, though," said Atticus as he rubbed his jaw.

Pito grinned, then frowned. He grabbed some of his belongings. Finding his communicator belt, he called for assistance from other raiders. When Pito reached the opening of the caverns, a light cycle bomber was at the opening.

Suddenly, the other raiders crossed their arms. Atticus was trailing Pito, and he could tell Pito was surprised by the look on his face. Atticus put himself up against the wall so Pito could not see him.

"What are you doing," said Pito to the raiders.

"Caldir, our new leader, does not want you with us anymore, Pito. Outsiders taint you, and they know your secret: You are not truly one of us," said a raider.

"Caldir can take that up with the other warlords," said Pito.

The other raiders blocked Pito's path with ion bars. Atticus pulled his ion gun from his side. *They were about to strike Pito*, he thought.

Once Atticus heard the Ion gun charging, he turned into full view of the cavern opening and fired several shots at the raiders, taking them down instantly. Running up to Pito, he saw Pito clutching his chest. He was not hit.

"You could have hit me! But instead, you saved me! Why?" said Pito.

"We both know the rules of how rough life can get, especially here on Y'Fert. I need a favor from you in the future," said Atticus.

The Pedisax accompanied Atticus to a remote spot in the desert, rarely visited by anyone. Cloths covered Pito and Atticus's faces as the sand blew fiercely around them and agitated the hodit. They set up camp with the Pedisax, and then Atticus went to a large dune.

Here, the wind and sand careened over giant dunes, forming flat areas as they spilled down the slopes. Frequented only by the native animals, insects, and avians of Y'Fert, the structure the group was looking at was an old Kernanite Fleet cruiser. Atticus began to walk towards the dilapidated cruiser. He waved at the Pedisax to come over and remove some of the metal. Atticus was at the part where the command center was exposed to the weather.

"What little we can get here, we may need," said Atticus.

"The raiders forbade this place to enter. They say it is haunted and is a sacred resting place for the souls lost in the Green Wars," said Pito.

Atticus brushed his comment aside as he rummaged and took what he could from the cruiser. It looked like it was fully equipped with weapons as Atticus went over the different consoles, which survived time and the elements.

After cutting and loosening some cords and equipment, Atticus gave a loud celebrant yell. He had found what he was looking for in the wreckage.

"What is it?" said Pito.

"It's a transponder," said Atticus.

"What can you use it for?" said Pito.

"I'm figuring I could use the transponder to detect the Kernanite Fleet. People say it was impossible, but that was until Llub found smaller and less intricate transponders in the Kernanite scouts that attacked," said Atticus.

"Why do we need to detect the Fleet," said Pito.

"We need to detect the Kernanite Fleet to save our home," said Atticus.

"But, Y'Fert is our home," said Pito.

Atticus glared at him. Pito looked bewildered. Measuring up Pito, Atticus went the other direction despite his body language signaling an imminent fight. As Atticus trailed off into the distance, Pito noticed he was humming a song. It was an old galactic song. He somehow remembered it.

Walking through the derelict cruise, Atticus saw more transponders. *We could finally detect the Kernanite Fleet even if they start to hide in space*, thought Atticus. Atticus heard a Pedisax warning call and looked up to see what it was. It looked like a vast sandstorm was approaching.

When Atticus returned to the *hodit*, Pito was typing on one of the holographic notebooks from the Star Jumper. Pito shut it off and looked back towards the mountains and hills where the dust storm appeared to come from in the distance.

When Pito, Atticus, and the Pedisax returned to camp and the Star Jumper, it was night, and Aida, Reno, and Llub were warming themselves by a fire. Pito and Atticus, wearied by travel, took their seating spaces around the fire. Atticus put the transponders on a table beside him.

"So, what's new?" said Captain Reno.

"Nothing, it seems. It looks like junk," said Aida.

Llub snarled at the two of them, then picked up the transponders. He eyed them carefully, then took a scanner at them. His eyes widened.

"My intuition was right. Atticus would never bring back junk. This seems like our ticket off this rock and forward with our journey," said Llub.

"But, this place is our home," said Reno.

Aida looked like she was becoming emotional. She looked over at where Sicro was buried. Looking away from the others, she got up and turned around to them.

"I have no feelings for this place anymore. That's all," said Aida.

Pito was looking around at the others, hoping Atticus would get a clue and introduce them to him. They all seemed preoccupied with something. He could not figure out what it was that kept entering their thoughts. Pito coughed loudly, and Atticus looked over at him.

"This is Pito. He's a raider who decided to attack us and revealed himself as my brother! Can you believe it?" said Atticus.

Atticus' exclamation was met with silence. No one in the group seemed enthralled that Pito was here. Captain Reno analyzed Pito for a bit. He suddenly gasped. Pito's skin began to glow a bluish hue.

"Look, Aida and Atticus! He's glowing like you two do!" said Llub.

"Who is the enemy this time?" Llub asked. With laughter, Llub pointed at Captain Reno and started to walk back to the desert floor.

"So, Captain Reno is the enemy?" said Atticus with laughter.

Pito blushed. He brought out a scanner to recheck the surrounding areas to ensure no raiders, wild animals, or possible attackers were present.

"So, back to the junk—I am figuring they are transponders of some sort," said Llub.

"Indeed," said Captain Reno, "Transponders like that can detect, hide anything, and communicate efficiently and quickly."

"Tomorrow, we will leave for Y'Fert," Atticus suddenly announced.

Captain Reno wanted to interject, but Atticus held his hand up in a halting way. Aida threw some sticks into the fire and drank clean river water. She looked over her glowing skin.

The morning after Pito's introduction, Atticus and the group began gathering the belongings they had added over the years. Captain Reno gave directions to some Pedisax on how to keep the farm. Llub started to say goodbye to some Pedisax hunters he had grown in friendship with. Atticus and Pito made some arrangements to ensure the farm and the Pedisax access to the water were safe from the raiders. Aida was in the Star Jumper making her bed in the passenger section. She looked unphased by the parting from Y'Fert.

Several days passed until the crew of the Star Jumper was ready. Each of them slowly entered the Star Jumper, and all said their goodbyes for one last time. Llub took it to the pilot's chair, and Atticus took it to the co-pilot's chair.

"Ready to make some history?" said Atticus.

Llub gave a deep, satisfied Itorian grin. His hands swiped over the pilot's console, and the Star Jumper moved upward quickly. Some Pedisax in the distance were seen waving goodbye. Once out of orbit from Y'Fert, Llub prepared to go to hyperspace to Stie Lux. Llub hit the hyperspace panel.

"Ready?" said Llub to Atticus.

"Ready!" said Atticus.

The Star Jumper blasted off to hyperspace. Most of the time, the crew ate and slept. Pito was the only one interested in anything, as everything was new.

"Atticus?" said Pito.

"Yes," replied Atticus.

"What is an X3 Scanner?" said Pito.

"Did you touch it? Don't tell me you touched it. It helps calibrate the hyperspace drive," said Atticus.

"Oh," said Pito. He withheld the X3 Scanner behind his back as he stood beside Atticus in the co-pilot's chair. His eyes filled with amazement, and he darted back and forth at all the coordinates and positions.

"I know what you can do. You can take the transponders we found and fit a couple of them into the Star Jumper's operational systems. We will need the Kernanite shadow technology to hide us once we are near Stie Lux," said Atticus.

Pito went over to where the transponders were and grabbed a couple of them. When he did, he passed by an ornate box. He touched it. Immediately, he felt a jolt of energy in him. *What is it?* He thought.

"Be careful!" said a voice behind him. It was Llub. He had recently finished dinner.

"What is it, Captain Reno? It's like it started to read my thoughts and had some power to it," said Pito.

"It's the Chalice of Life from the planet Mond-Qu," said Captain Reno Bahm.

"The Chalice of Life? The one who grants immortality," said Pito.

"Yup," said Llub, "That's the one."

Pito tapped the box again. It shook and glowed a bit. He looked around the Star Jumper and at Reno. His eyes glimmered with intrigue.

Aida came over and slammed her right hand next to the box. Pito jumped and took a step back from Aida and the box. Captain Bahm smiled and noted Aida's sudden appearance.

"What do you think you are doing?" demanded Aida.

Pito looked up at a stern-looking Aida. She had her hand on her hips, and her eyes looked intense. Llub briefly looked away at the display of anger.

"He was just looking at it?" said Captain Reno.

"Well, everyone has agreed that the Chalice of Life is too precious to handle for now. Maybe we could find it a home when we get to Stie Lux," said Aida.

To Pito, the Chalice of Life already had some magical hold over him. *It was magical, alright*, thought Pito. He continued to touch and then finger the fine artwork outside the box. Aida rolled her eyes.

The control consoles along the hulls of the Star Jumper glimmered with data from the Stie Lux star system. Captain Bahm went to the consoles to adjust the data collection. For a while, the Star Jumper experienced intermittent shaking, which would be described as turbulence if it were in the air.

"We're dropping out of hyperspace, everyone. Please get to your stations," Llub said over the communicator.

As soon as everyone knew, they came out of hyperspace and went to Stie Lux. Looking at their view screens, the crew of the Star Jumper noticed something off about Stie Lux. It was noted that it was the dark side of the planet they were looking at.

"I'm scanning the planet's surface. So far, the planet is in some information loop. It is not willing to transfer information out," said Atticus.

"The lights are also out on Stie Lux. Is anyone home?" said Llub

"We'll find out," said Atticus.

XVII

The Star Jumper plunged into darkness while the whooshing sound of air filled the ship's interior. Atticus gripped the co-pilot's seat tightly. Looking over at Llub, he saw an intense concern and determination in his companion's eyes. The Star Jumper took a plunge along with Atticus' stomach. Aida let out a scream, and Captain Reno looked for a sedative. All this motion entertained Pito. Atticus looked at Pito. By the looks of it, it looked as if he was riding a hodit back on Y'Fert.

The view screen blinked on and off, showing a possible landing site on the nearest flat land. Atticus closed his eyes, and his body tightened. Then, he heard the Star Jumper touching the ground.

"Well, that was a joy ride," said Llub.

"You could have made it a little softer landing," glared Atticus.

When Atticus stepped out of the Star Jumper, a fog whipped around his feet. They had landed on a coastal plain near an ocean. The clouds were purple as the twin moons of Stie Lux cast their light on the sea and plain below them. Atticus took his thumb to the twin moons to measure and see if the tides had come in for the night. It looked like they had come in about two hours ago from their position. He remembered that, in his childhood, he freshly cooked fish and seaweed for breakfast. It would be daylight in a couple of hours. Atticus turned to the others.

"It would be best to make our way to the capital of Tonbre," said Atticus.

Aida shivered as the warmth of the ocean briefly turned into cold. She had never been in a world like this before in her life. From the stories she was told about it, it was enchanted.

"Are we safe, though, Atticus?" said Aida.

"The transponders performed its shadow technology well. The Kernanite Fleet here did not detect us," said Atticus.

"Llub also did some excellent flying," said Captain Bahm.

Pito had gone off to the side of the group to look towards the sea. He looked mesmerized by something. Atticus walked over and grabbed him by the shoulder.

"This is our home. We can liberate it from the Kernanites," said Atticus to Pito.

"But why would the local population listen to you and me, Atticus? We are nothing but sons of forgotten rulers," said Pito.

"We have nothing to lose, Pito, by gaining their attention," said Atticus.

In the forest behind the crew, they heard bushes and leaves resettling. Everyone in the group got their ion guns ready. Aida went to the back of the group towards the Star Jumper. What popped out from behind the shrubbery was a rotund, highly adorned Netcaz.

"Hello, there," said the Netcaz.

Atticus signaled the others to stand and put their weapons at their sides. He remembered the Netcaz from his childhood. They were a native population of foragers and builders of three cities. They were isolative but friendly simultaneously, and no one knew why.

"Hello! What's your name? And, if you don't mind me asking, what are you doing here?" said Atticus.

"I'm Riceub of the Netcaz. I'm on a scouting mission to see where the lights came from in the sky. Now, I know they were from your ship," said Riceub.

"Have you seen anyone from the Kernanite Fleet?" said Atticus.

"None," said Riceub. Riceub looked concerned at the question and noticed the others, especially Aida, in the background.

"You have a Humar with you," said Riceub.

"Yes, we do," said Atticus.

Riceub looked puzzled. He scratched his head and then looked at a scanner he held with his big hands and long fingers. The scanner started to beep, and Riceub moved towards the Star Jumper. Captain Reno held out his arm to block him.

"What are you doing?" said Riceub.

"We cannot let you on the Star Jumper," said Reno.

"But why? The scanner is picking up a power signature of some kind," said Riceub.

Atticus put his hand on Riceub's shoulder, but then suddenly, Atticus' tattoo began to glow. He pulled back from Riceub, but it was too late. A surge of energy jettisoned Atticus to the bushes. Aida ran over, and her skin was glowing as well. Riceub looked horrified at what had just happened.

"You are Humar, and that one looks Stie Luxian," said Riceub. The puzzled look on Riceub continued. The dots on the Netcaz's face jump from point to point as he converses with Atticus. Aida came up from the Star Jumper to Atticus' side. Riceub shoved Aida to the side.

"Stupid, Humar, and all their tricks," said Riceub.

"Their kind is saving us during this war," said Atticus to the Netcaz.

Riceub scoffed and continued with his duty of scanning the Star Jumper. Aida rubbed her shoulder, and Atticus quickly went to Llub. Llub seemed preoccupied with something else.

"Atticus, I'm not sure about Stie Lux," said Llub.

"What do you mean?" said Atticus.

"This Netcaz is coming off the wrong way. They should be more—friendly," said Llub.

"Well, Llub, diplomacy was never your strength," said Atticus. Llub smiled and went over to chat with Captain Reno. Atticus wanted to bring up who he was to Riceub the Netcaz to see if that would get him anywhere.

"You know, I never did introduce myself. I'm Atticus," he said.

For a moment, Netcaz ignored him, then abruptly turned around to face Atticus. He pointed in the direction from which he had come through the forest. Pito looked in Riceub's direction and found lights coming their way.

"Tonbre is that way along with the rest of you invasive, overlord scum," said Riceub.

"Who's that coming?" said Pito.

"If your friend is who he says he is, they'll either be furious or ecstatic," said Riceub.

"Let's meet them halfway in the forest," said Pito to Atticus and Captain Reno.

"It looks like a crowd of people heading our way," said Riceub.

Atticus leads the way through the forest with the others behind him. The lights from the crowd grew brighter with every step he took towards them. He decided to go around them to see if they could move away from them and walk towards the city. It was too late.

"You there! Stop!" said a loud voice.

Ion energy shots soon filled the forest, and Atticus returned fire. Captain Reno joined the fight. An ion grenade went off somewhere to Atticus' left.

"Riceub! Do something!" said Atticus.

Riceub touched his utility belt and looked through his choices of weapons. Instantly, a net appeared around Atticus, Captain Reno, and Riceub, stunning the entire crowd.

A dense fog began to roll through as Atticus, Reno, and Riceub rummaged through the crowd, looking for clues as to why they were attacked. One of the attackers started to wake up, and Reno head-butted him to the ground. Reaching into the jacket of the last attacker, Atticus found what he was looking for in the fallen attacker.

"They're from the Army of the Chalice of Life," said Atticus.

"Give me that!" said Riceub.

The Netcaz poured over the details of the attacker's badge. He smiled as he clicked open the badge, revealing energy pulsating from it. Riceub took his scanner and smiled no more.

"They are from the Army of the Chalice of Life from the energy signatures in this badger. I thought they were only a myth. Even here on Stie Lux, no one seriously talked about the Army," said Riceub.

Some tree branches rustled behind Riceub. Atticus pointed his ion weapon. It was Aida, Llub, and Pito. Aida and Llub were carrying something between them with a cloth over it.

"What did you bring?" said Atticus.

"We brought the Chalice of Life," said Aida.

"We thought you may need some help when we heard the attacks," said Pito.

"Well, unless you want to go through the trouble of stunning them again, we better hurry to the city," said Riceub.

"Understood," said Llub.

Atticus took the lead, trudging through the thick forest to Tonbre. When they got there, they stumbled upon what looked like a celebration. Fireworks filled the air, and revelers were on the street. Pito went to Atticus' side.

"We go to an inn of some sort," said Pito.

"Agreed," said Atticus.

Riceub never once took his scanner off the Chalice of Life box. Atticus occasionally would look back at him with a frown. They eventually found a place to rest. It was called the Galactic Lodge.

"A room for five," said Atticus.

"What are you bringing to Tonbre—a circus?" said the lodge-keeper.

Stie Luxians were insular people who were fiercely attached to their freedom. They did not like the influence of outsiders. Over the years, though, the Stie Luxians forgot the ways of their rulers long ago. After all, they did not know that several were in their midst.

Everyone slept under a roof that night as the nightly revelers walked past the lodge. Occasionally, a *nibit*—a native hound dog howled in the night. When Atticus was sound asleep, he heard the lodge door falling open and hitting the floor. He ran from his room only to find more men with weapons. They were from the General's Guard. Their golden uniforms glowed in the moonlight.

"We're looking for Atticus Lokar. There is an order for his arrest from General Pox," said one of the soldiers.

The General's Guard was neither an army of soldiers nor warriors. They were in place for the eventual return of the rulers of Stie Lux. Atticus squinted at the light beamed on his face and coughed as the dust filled his lungs.

"There is no one here by that name," said Atticus.

"His family is a group of criminals—nothing more. And, who are you?" said a soldier.

"My name is Menco. I'm from a village on the coast," said Atticus.

The soldiers frowned. Atticus did not know what to do now. They did not seem to buy his story. A soldier brought out one of his scanners and went to where the lodge attendant was sleeping. A scuffle was heard, and the soldier returned bloodied but with the attendant.

"That's him, that's Atticus Lokar," said the lodge attendant.

Atticus' tattoo began to glow immediately, and he held up his arm just in time to block a shot from one of the soldiers. The energy shield he developed around his body absorbed the shot. Llub woke up to what was happening and attempted to pull out his ion gun, but he was stunned quickly. The soldiers grabbed Llub. Atticus let the blue energy build up in his hand and jettisoned a volley at the Guard. Some fell, but they ran too quickly, dragging Llub.

Atticus ran back to the others. Aida, Pito, and Reno were at the doors to their rooms. The soldiers were heard moaning, and the lodge attendant yelled for them to leave his lodge.

"What do we do, Atticus?" said Reno.

"We need to teleport the Chalice back to the Star Jumper," said Atticus.

"But we need it to save Stie Lux," said Aida.

"It looks like there is a fight for who controls this planet before we save it. Pito, do you have enough power on your scanner to teleport the Chalice?" said Atticus.

"I do," said Pito.

"Then do it! And, teleport yourself too," said Atticus.

Atticus and everyone made their way out of the lodge through the windows. Rovers of the Guard filled the streets and made their way around the borders of Tonbre. Atticus was bringing up the group's tail when his foot was caught beneath the root of a tree.

"Atticus, what are you doing?" said Captain Reno.

"I'm stuck! Go ahead of me!" said Atticus.

A rover was heard coming towards them, and Reno grabbed his ion gun but was stunned. Before Atticus knew it, the Guards were everywhere. The last thing he remembers was the moist earth of the forest.

Atticus woke up on a stone-made floor. The cold air from the morning seemed through one window. The morning sunlight poured through it, exposing a slimy and wet cell. Seeing Llub in the corner of the cell, Atticus kicked over a bucket to wake Llub.

"Llub, it's me, Atticus," he said.

Llub rolled over and then rolled over to where Atticus was in the cell. He had several bruises on his arms, but he was otherwise healthy. A General's Guard was placed outside the cell door. By the looks of the emblem on the General's Guard, they were inside the citadel of General Pox.

Atticus found a chip in his right sleeve. The shackles holding him were operated chips, so Atticus decided to pick the lock. It took about three tries, but Atticus got his shackles off.

He did the same thing with Llub. Examining the door, Atticus knew he needed an explosive to open the door. He found an old scanner in his utility belt that he could explode. He was surprised he had one. The Guard did not fully disarm him. Atticus and Llub stepped back to the other side of the cell. The scanner exploded. Immediately, a Guard appeared, and Atticus disarmed him with a punch. He grabbed his weapons.

Looking around the hallway, Atticus surmised they were right below the Ruler's Room.

It took some time for Atticus and Llub to make their way to the Ruler's Room. It looked like no one was there. Lighting orbs lit as they walked through the chamber. The final orb lit, and then they saw General Pox sitting on the throne with a box and a cloth. It was the Chalice of Life. Somehow, he had obtained. Atticus and Llub glanced around, but before they could pull their weapons, the General's Guard put knives to their throat.

General Pox clapped his hands and removed the cloth. The Chalice glowed, and the Ruler's Tiara was next to it. General Pox summoned more Guards, and they brought Aida and the rest with them.

"Well done, everyone, for following into the enemy's hand," said General Pox.

"So, the great, mighty Atticus has come for his throne. From where? Ah, you are coming from Fina. The unlikely home to the galaxy's forgotten," said General Pox.

"Let everyone go and just take me," exclaimed Atticus.

"General, we have movement around the orbit of Stie Lux. It's the Kernanites, General," said a soldier.

Atticus and Aida, among others, felt the blue energy flow through them again. Aida tried to shake her way out of the hands of a Guard, but she failed. Atticus did as well. Their energy only grew more powerful as the guards shielded their eyes.

XVIII

General Pox and the Guard blocked their eyes from the light. They hit the floor. The Ruler's Tiara rose from its place. It shone brightly. Some of the soldiers attempted to grab it but were repelled. Aida's skin began to glow the iridescent blue. Atticus began punching his way through as many guards as possible. Running toward the Ruler's Tiara, Aida placed it on her head. Blazing light came forth from the tiara. The guards began to run away in fear.

Atticus noticed some blood on his arm, but he got lucky. His tattoo was also glowing. He wanted to go after General Pox. Pito and the others were holding their fight with the guards.

By the time Atticus got to where General Pox was, the General teleported and shimmered out of the Ruler's Room. Riceub was busy coordinating new ways to get out of the dangerous situation. He worked frantically.

"Atticus," said Riceub, "The Kernanites began to attack Stie Lux and Tonbre. It is only a matter of time before the planet and the city falls to them."

Aida ran over to the throne in the Ruler's Room and looked at her new place. Two Kernanite warships could be seen above the capital. The capital, however, was struck by ion bombs now and then.

Atticus looked back at the rest of the group. Llub was helping Captain Reno up from the floor. For some reason, Aida went to the throne with her skin glowing. Pito looked like he was moving the Chalice of Life, but it looked stuck in its box. Riceub gazed out of the window with Atticus.

"Well, Atticus, you made it to your ancestral home. Now, what?" said Riceub.

"It looks like I imagined it—even the Ruler's Room looks like it was just yesterday my mother and father left from Stie Lux," said Atticus.

"This place suits you, Atticus. There is fun in town and a bunch of people to order around here," said Llub.

"That brings to mind Riceub. How will we get the General's Guard on our side?" said Atticus.

"They announced that the Kernanites were here, so they would be around the major cities and the coasts," said Riceub.

"We should send out encryption codes to lock the Guard from their weapons," said Captain Reno.

"That is a marvelous idea," said Riceub.

"We need to get back to the Star Jumper before more bombs fall on Tonbre," said Llub.

"Wait, I can't go with you," said Aida.

Atticus ran over to Aida. She looked tired. Her glowing skin seemed to overtake the other lights near her. The blue light shone upon Atticus, and it calmed him.

"We cannot stay here, Aida. We must go," said Atticus.

"Atticus! The coastal villages and plains are starting to burn. I'll alert the Netcaz. They live in the forest on the other side of the city," Riceub.

Captain Reno and Llub followed Riceub. Pito was still fixated on the Chalice. It looked like he did not want to leave it.

"Pito, we must go," said Atticus.

"The secret though, Atticus. And, we cannot let it fall into enemy hands," said Pito.

The citadel began to shake as Kernanite warships targeted Tonbre. Screams from city dwellers were heard from the streets. Aida was staring straight forward across the Ruler's Room without a blink in her eye.

Atticus grabbed Aida, picked her up, and walked across the Ruler's Room. She let out a gasp. The Chalice of Life still caught Pito's attention. Atticus bumped him on his shoulder to signal that it was time to leave.

Pito snapped out of it and grabbed the Chalice of Life. The group made their way through the maze-like citadel. When they came to the streets, they found horror everywhere. Children were left without parents, and the old were left alone to die. The Stie Luxians knew the end must be near to go so low and without a fight. Some of the General's Guards were seen in the distance.

Everyone brought out their ion weapon but hid in an alleyway to let them pass. Riceub was sweating and breathing hard. Captain Reno and Llub moved to the other side of the alleyway to show that the way was clear.

"We must make it to the forest. My people can help Atticus and Aida," said Riceub.

"With what? Stie Lux is under attack," said Captain Reno. Riceub smiled. Captain Reno smirked back at him.

"We'll try this," said Riceub.

Riceub searched through his utility belt, and suddenly, a transporter doorway opened. Dust began to fall from buildings around them as they shook. Riceub took Aida by the hand. After everyone entered the teleportation door, Atticus stopped and looked at Riceub.

"I want to thank you for everything you have done," said Atticus.

Before Atticus could finish what he was saying, some General's Guards appeared in the alleyway and loaded their weapons. With one shot, they hit Riceub, and he was killed. Atticus knelt to check Riceub's pulse, but there was nothing he could do—he was dead.

Atticus quickly went through the teleportation doorway, and in a moment, he was by the Star Jumper with the others. Llub immediately closed the teleportation doorway behind Atticus. The trees along the coast began to sway as a storm rolled across the plain.

"Did Riceub make it?" said Captain Reno.

Atticus just shook his head.

"Damn it," said Captain Reno, "He was our way out of here!"

Atticus walked over to the Star Jumper—exhausted. The others made their way into the Star Jumper. Llub sat down beside Atticus.

"I want you to go ahead of me, Atticus. I'll be fine," said Llub.

"But—you won't make it, Llub—Tonbre and the planet are swarming with Kernanites," said Atticus.

"It's for the best and the best for the galaxy. And, Aida," said Llub.

"What will you do? How will you help us?" said Atticus.

"I found a Netcaz Star Jumper orbiting Stie Lux. We could have Captain Reno and Pito pilot it and man it. They will give you cover from the Kernanites in case they overrun you," said Llub.

"I'll be conducting operations from a citadel outside a town on the other coast," said Llub.

"Alright, stay safe," said Atticus.

The yellow and orange fire from the ion weapons burned across the Sti Luxian sky. Tonbre was in flames. A dark cloud of smoke covered the two moons while Llub went to the other side of the coast.

"Atticus, what is Llub doing?" said Aida.

"He's providing more backup," said Atticus.

"Atticus, this is Captain Reno. I am engaging the shadow cloak, and we will be in orbit shortly," said Captain Reno.

Aida was groaning in pain. She was itching her skin, and the Ruler's Tiara was still on her head. Atticus thought she looked beautiful in it. It looked as good on her as it did his mother.

When the Star Jumper reached orbit, everyone looked out at the mayhem unleashed by the Kernanites. The Stie Luxian Fleet was enabled and had engaged the Kernanites. Some groups of Netcaz fighters were seen as well.

"They are given it all they got to fight off the Kernanites," said Atticus to Aida

Atticus looked at his tattoo, which was still glowing, and then at Aida. He went to the operations console to see if he could pick up any signal of Ba'Gam. Operations came back with no signal of Ba'Gam. Atticus sighed.

"Atticus, we have spotted the Netcaz Star Jumper," said Captain Reno.

"On it," said Atticus.

It only took about an hour or two for Pito and Captain Reno to switch between the Star Jumper and the Netcaz ship. Atticus was in the transferring hub between the two Star Jumpers when a blaze of light was seen coming from around Stie Lux. Atticus only thought a warship exploded. More explosions occurred, and then he felt the Star Jumper's spinning.

"We got a problem, Atticus," said Captain Reno.

"The Kernanites have used ion colliders to bombard the surface of Stie Lux," said Pito.

"Atticus, are you there?" said Captain Reno.

Atticus was running and vomiting at the same time. The energy waves released by the ion colliders sent the Star Jumpers spinning. *What had happened to Llub?* thought Atticus.

Atticus sat back in the pilot's chair and released the Star Jumper from the Netcaz ship. Aida went to the science console to see what they looked at from the viewscreen. Shockwaves continued to rock the Netcaz ship.

"Atticus, Stie Lux is rubble. It's gone, Atticus," said Aida.

"What?" said Atticus.

"We need to get out of here. Chunks of Stie Lux are coming in our direction," said Aida.

The Netcaz ship did a roll and released itself from the Star Jumper. Glowing pieces of rock zoomed past the two ships. The Star Jumper engaged its engines and flew past the debris. The Netcaz ship trailed them.

"Atticus, what happened to Llub? We need to jump to hyperspace. There is part of the Kernanite Fleet ahead of us," said Captain Reno.

Atticus was trying to get his bearings inside the Star Jumper and to see if he could pick up Llub's signal. The Star Jumper dropped out of space at the solar system's edge. Taking readings of what Stie Lux was, I see that there was no way Llub could have made it. He was gone.

He sat back in his chair. Aida did not look so well, so he asked a medical robot to assess them. The cold fingers of the robot dashed across Atticus' arm.

"You do not look well," said the medical robot.

"You are going through a state of shock from all the stress—Aida, as well," said the robot.

Atticus held back tears. They were so close to stopping the Kernanites. He could feel it, but they had lost Stie Lux—his home and everyone living on it. He poured over the new data to see if there was any sign of Ba'Gam's ship. There was nothing.

Captain Reno's Netcaz ship dropped out of hyperspace near Atticus. Atticus did not feel like talking to them. *What about D'Er?* thought Atticus. He began to figure Ba'Gaam was after something even more frightening than destroying Stie Lux.

"Atticus, we need to move it before more rocky debris gets us from the destruction of Stie Lux," said Reno.

"Where do you suggest we go to," said Atticus to Reno.

"We need to go back to Y'Fert," said Reno.

"Why?" said Atticus.

"The Chalice—it's holding Pito in some trance. How is Aida?" said Reno.

"A medical robot is taking care of her," said Atticus.

Atticus stared at the sensors as they picked up more and more debris. He felt overwhelmed by it all. Many lives were lost potentially because of his inadequacies. *Was he not who the galaxy said he was?* he thought.

"I need to head to Y'Fert to see the Pedisax," said Reno.

Atticus did not know what to say to Captain Reno. It seemed like everything was falling apart on this journey. Then he thought about it. Whatever Pito and Aida are going through is probably connected to D'Er. Even though the planet was long ago forgotten, it still had a worthy place in the galaxy as the home of Atticus' family.

He began plugging in the coordinates for D'Er. He put in more orders to the medical robots to assist Aida. He waited for Captain Reno to give him the signal.

"Atticus, we have no enemies in site for our separation," said Reno.

"Gotcha, Captain Reno," said Atticus.

They both launched their ships into hyperspace. Atticus sat beside Aida as she lay on a medical bay bed with her eyes closed and her breathing was shallow. Her skin continued to glow. Atticus looked at his tattoo and knew his had not stopped shining since arriving on Stie Lux.

"It's a mystery why you and Aida's unique traits remain active," said the medical robot.

"Tell me something I don't know," retorted Atticus. He hit the bulkhead of the Star Jumper. They were heading to D'Er whether he liked it or not. A thousand thoughts crossed his mind. *What would Llub do in this situation?* he thought. He had always felt Llub had the right solutions despite his pedigree. Now, he will never see him again.

Atticus tossed and turned on a lumpy bed in the pilot's cabin of the Star Jumper. Aida was sleeping in the medical room when a sensor went off in the command center. Atticus rolled out of bed—groggily. He took a swig of some *zeti* juice while he stared in disbelief. Half of the Kernanite fleet was trailing him and heading toward D'Er.

He tried to communicate with Captain Reno, but his attempts failed. There was too much interference. He scanned the region again. It was too late. More Kernanite warships were almost on top of Captain Reno. The Netcaz ship had some firepower and good shields, though. Captain Reno could hold them off until they go to the surface.

Pulling himself together again, he thought about the hyperspace engines. He could supercharge them to accelerate them further to D'Er. There was a shot they would get Ba'Gam. He had lost almost everyone on this journey, on this fool's errand to avoid their fate with the Kernanites.

Captain Reno was a tough soldier and warrior but was not much of a match for Ba'Gam and the rest of the fleet. Atticus settled down again for the night. He sent a message to Captain Reno, hoping it would be received before dropping out of hyperspace at Y'Fert.

Looking at Pito, Captain Reno gave him another eye scan. Nothing showed up on the scan; he was healthy. Pito continued to stare forward, fixated on the Chalice. After doing more and more scans of the Chalice, the energy signatures only led to one place—Y'Fert. What was there, Captain Reno did not know.

He was in the mess hall when a message arrived. It was encrypted and sent from Atticus one day ago.

"Captain Reno, this is Atticus. If you receive this message, you made it or—almost. Half of the Kernanite fleet is following me, and the other half is going after you," said Atticus.

Captain Reno immediately went to his sensors. The Netcaz ship had come to a complete stop and was orbiting Y'Fert. Reno sent out a message to the Pedisax about his arrival. The vessel remained in shadow while Captain Reno waited. The Kernanite Fleet was orbiting as well. It looked like the fight had now come to Y'Fert. Pito then suddenly got up from the floor and then fell into an unconscious state.

XIX

Atticus pressed the button to engage the hyperspace engines. He sat back in the pilot's chair. He closed his eyes and thought of Fina for a time. He had not thought about Fina throughout their journey. He believed it would only hold them back, but after the destruction of Stie Lux, he felt a need to reminiscence. He had not forgotten Fina's beauty or its people's welcoming atmosphere and warmth. Atticus wondered more profoundly what it all meant and whether or not they would stop Ba'Gam and the Kernanites.

The Star Jumper zoomed through the galaxy. Atticus was in the Star Jumper's exercise room when one of the medical robots began to malfunction. He hopped off the exercise bike in the corner of the room.

He brought some tools from the mechanic room on the deck below the main one. *If anything, more could go wrong, it may*, briefly thought Atticus. One medical robot was obsolete this far out in the galaxy. Aida would occasionally try to get up, but it was too painful.

The sensors finally went off, showing that the ship had reached D'Er's system. They would drop out of hyperspace on the orbit of D'Er. A thud was heard as the Star Jumper coasted out of hyperspace. Atticus then saw the D'Er; it was as beautiful as he had heard back in Fina. The green, greyish clouds contrasted with blue, crystalline seas. A warm, deep green stretched for miles on land. D'Er had only one moon, and it was barren. The people of D'Er colonized the moon for thousands of years before its abandonment.

Atticus turned the Star Jumper's shadow cloak to hide them. He positioned himself so they would orbit above the main continent to fly to Craigo, a small city known for having D'Er artifacts. Atticus planned to leave Aida on the Star Jumper with the last medical robots while he searched for an answer. He sent a message down to the surface so he would not arrive announced.

The people of Craigo looked weird to Atticus. They dressed out of fashion, even for people on D'Er, and the looks on their faces were disconnected. Some of the traders gave Atticus looks of suspicion. And some even jeered at him.

"Who are you? A claimant? A bandit from the Rim," said someone.

"You deserve nothing," another said.

And another spat on Atticus.

A lot had changed over the decades on Craigo. Some cities lay abandoned, but Ba'Gam and the rest of the Kernanites were not simply after a place; they were after someone—they were after Atticus. Atticus followed a trail up to a nearby mountain where a waterfall fell.

Craigo had so far yielded nothing. He washed his hands in a pool of water and suddenly heard the sound in the air. The sound of Kernanite fighters. They were here. Atticus ran to Craigo and found a priest who was running from the bombs.

"Tell me, Man of the Light, where are you going?" said Atticus.

"I am going to worship for the last time," said the priest. The priest stared intently at Atticus. He touched his face.

"You are Atticus," said the priest.

"Yes—Yes, I am," said Atticus.

"They are after you for the right to rule the galaxy, but they cannot. The war will only end once you give it your all. I must go," said the priest.

The priest ran into the distant alleyways of Craigo. Atticus looked at his tattoo. It glowed and shone so much he had to put his coat over it. Ba'Gam was here. Ba'Gam was here to finish what he started, but Atticus was ready.

* * *

Captain Reno teleported Pito, the Chalice, and himself to the encampment where Sicro was buried. He sent a message to the Pedisax, who were waiting for him. The Pedisax looked relieved he was here.

"Captain Reno, no words can describe how glad we are to see you! We have held our oath to what is left of your long stay here on Y'Fert," said a Pedisax.

"Very good," said Reno.

"But, my friend Pito—Atticus' brother—he's sick. It has something to do with the Chalice. We thought, but now he has fallen out of the chance and unconscious," said Reno.

The Pedisax shaman took his staff out and held it over Pito. Nothing happened. The Pedisax looked frustrated and then went over to the Chalice.

"This is troubling. It seems an evil force is behind this, and the Chalice is barely holding Pito together," said the shaman.

"Did anything bad happen recently here?" said Captain Reno.

"Some raiders were attempting to rob the grave of Sicro, but we repelled them," said a Pedisax warrior.

Captain Reno looked around the grave site for any clues. Someone among the raiders knew that Sicro was buried here. Reno found the clue in some burned wood near the grave site. It was the Kernanite emblem. It was someone powerful then.

"Caldir was here," said Reno.

The Pedisax sounded an alarm, and the warriors pointed and looked at the sky. Reno held his hands up to the sun. It was the Kernanites. They had launched their fighters and cruisers.

Captain Reno looked through his utility belt. He needed to transport Pito and the Chalice, but the signal would not lock on them. The Pedisax took their *hodit* and their group to the caverns. Suddenly, the Chalice began to float seamlessly in the air Sicro. Energy poured forth from the Chalice Siro's grave.

Pito let out a scream and fell again to the desert floor. He began to writhe in pain. Reno was frightened, so he grabbed the shaman by the shoulder.

"Please stay; I need you. I know very little about the spiritual world," said Captain Reno.

The shaman waved his staff over Sicro's grave and placed it on Pito's head. He mumbled many prayers to himself. He let his arms stretch out, allowing the sun to warm his body against the calm wind of the desert plain. Captain Reno looked on, and without warning, Sicro's grave began to open.

Sicro stumbled out in the funeral garb, shaking and confused. Pito stood up, eyes locked on Sicro with a wide-open stare. Captain Reno went over to Pito and put his arms around him. He tried to calm him.

"What happened? I felt the sun shining on my face; then I felt cold; then I felt warm sunshine," said Sicro.

Sicro looked at Reno briefly before touching the ground frantically.

"Is this Y'Fert? Who are you?" said Sicro, pointing to Pito.

"This is indeed Y'Fert," said the shaman.

"Pito, this is Atticus' son, your nephew," said Captain Reno.

* * *

Kernanite soldiers marched up and down the streets and alleyways of Craigo. Cries from townspeople were heard all over Craigo. It made Atticus seethe with fury. These people were his people; he just knew.

Craigo was positioned on a cliff overlooking what locals called "the god's lake." Atticus stood atop one of the cliff walls far from the city center. He managed to find a path that led to a remote outcrop.

Atticus sat on the other side of the outcrop. He was relieved he had found a hiding place from the troops until he heard faint whispers—and as he got close, they sounded like chanting. Atticus readied his ion weapon but then charged it down, as he was now looking at the same priest he had met in Craigo.

"Wh—at are you doing here?" said Atticus.

The priest smiled.

"I came here to say some prayers. This must be the work of the gods. I found you here, and they led you right back to me," said the priest.

"Yes—I am Atticus Lokar of the House of D'Er, son of General Atticus I," said Atticus.

The priest smiled even more brightly.

"Of course you are. My name is Nead, by the way," said the priest.

"What does who I am have to do with the fall of Craigo?" said Atticus.

"Ba'Gam is after legitimacy, as everyone now knows on D'Er. The other cities throughout the planet have put up a fight, but they cannot hold Ba'Gam off much more," said Nead.

"What kind of legitimacy is Ba'Gam searching for," said Atticus.

"If Ba'Gam cannot have you—and I sense someone else—he is going after something old," said Nead.

"Like what?" said Atticus.

Nead pointed behind him at what looked like caves, but given a closer look, they were ruins. Pillars jutted out over the lake. Trees swayed in the lakeside wind.

"It's one of your ancient palaces. It's nothing," laughed Nead.

Nead bit his lip, noticing Atticus did not return his laughter. Atticus' tattoo glowed, and it began to sting. Atticus fingered the ancient writings on the walls of the palace. Mural after ancient mural was covered in dust and moss. The ancient palace suddenly shook as distant ion bombs went off in Craigo.

Atticus sensed the palace was not just *nothing*. The priest was stressed from the Kernanites' attack. Atticus went back into the palace's labyrinth. Ancient rooms were filled with forgotten trinkets and ceremonial ware. In the far back of the palace, he came upon a room with an ornate ceiling. Light shone from windows way up in the room. It was majestic.

Atticus heard Nead following him. Nead coughed and began to open up a book. He looked teary-eyed almost as he sifted through the pages.

"This is where your mother and father were with their court before they died," said Nead.

"Did they leave any messages or anything behind?" said Atticus.

"There is an old saying, "He who rules rules with their right and left hand justly," said Nead.

Atticus furrowed his brow. There must be more to this story of his parents, but there was little time. Everything was quiet in the ancient palace, and then he heard the shifting of footsteps behind them toward the palace entrance.

"Get down," said Atticus to Nead.

"What is it? Who is it?" said Nead.

Atticus held his tattoo and ground his teeth. He was in pain. Ba'Gam was close. His tattoo told him so. But was it him?

Atticus got up and ready his ion weapon. Nead crouched behind a pillar, and Atticus gave him an ion gun. Nead just shook his head.

"I'm a priest. We do not take up arms against anyone. Friend or foe," said Nead.

Atticus smirked. "You said you knew my family? Now is the time to show it," said Atticus.

A loud explosion was heard inside the palace, and stones crumbled from its ceiling. Birds flew in every direction. Nead stood up and took a position next to Atticus.

"Atticus, my boy, where are you? It's been so long," said Ba'Gam.

Atticus did not want to give away his position, so he touched his utility belt to activate shadow technology to hide him and Nead. As soon as he did, Ba'Gam was seen in the distance.

Atticus motioned for Nead to hide among the other pillars across the room. Ba'Gam came forth. An ion gun was slung around his shoulder, and a book was held in his hand.

"You have what I want, Atticus," said Ba'Gam.

"I don't have what you are looking for—take your soldiers and leave D'Er," said Atticus.

Ba'Gam laughed. "Those are bold words for someone not in the position to give up his wife—his love," said Ba'Gam.

Atticus winced. They found Aida and the Star Jumper. He shot at Ba'Gam, only for shields to disperse the shot.

"Wherever you have gone, I have followed Atticus. I have followed you to far reaches of the galaxy if I have had to," said Ba'Gam.

"All for nothing," shouted Atticus.

Ba'Gam held up his finger. He smiled. And, then, he brought his ion weapon to point toward Nead.

Beads of sweat poured down Atticus. Ba'Gam had found Nead. Atticus then took a step into the light of the room.

Ba'Gam smiled again.

"You spared your friend—a priest, I see," said Ba'Gam.

Ba'Gam then shot his ion weapon at Nead. Nead fell to the floor. Atticus drew his gun and fired at Ba'Gam. Atticus rolled on the floor to the other side of the room where Nead was, and he checked to see if he was dead. He was only stunned.

"Next time, you won't be so lucky. But it is not you; I'm after the priest. I'm after Aida, the Chalice, and Atticus," said Ba'Gam.

Atticus crouched down along the pillar and looked through his teleporter module to see if he could locate Aida. She was somewhere at the front of the palace. Atticus stood and grabbed Nead's ion weapon.

Ba'Gam whistled, and the footsteps of soldiers were heard. Whimpering was heard in the darkness of the palace. Aida was then shoved in the light of the main room.

"You're all better now, Aida. I healed you," said Ba'Gam.

"You cannot heal what was never ill," said Aida.

"True. But I still want you. Now, take a seat on that throne towards the end of the main room," said Ba'Gam.

An ion bomb was heard going off, and more stones fell. Atticus knew there was not much time for Ba'Gam's plot with Aida because the palace may not stay intact. Aida took a seat where Ba'Gam told her.

Her tiara began to shine, and then a D'Er map appeared before Aida. Ba'Gam clapped his hands. He called more Kernanite warriors over to his side.

"So, I was right, Aida, you are my type. I will rule with you. The map has pointed to here. Here. Here was the last place Atticus's family ruled before the wars broke out all across the galaxy. And, here is where all the galaxy's power is held—in the bond between Aida and Atticus," said Ba'Gam.

"You can't have her. You can't have either of us," said Atticus.

Atticus charged at Ba'Gam, but before Atticus could reach him, one of the warriors took a shot at him and hit him to the floor. Aida screamed, and Ba'Gam hollered in jubilance. He grabbed the back of Atticus' neck and put his face on the floor.

"I'm about to smother you and your plot, Atticus," said Ba'Gaam.

"No, you're not," said a voice.

It was Nead.

Nead held an ion grenade and threw it at Ba'Gam—making it stick to his armor. Atticus then got up, threw Ba'Gam to the warriors, and ran and took Aida back behind the other pillars of the room. The grenade exploded.

Atticus went over to where Ba'Gam fell. He touched him. He was dead.

XX

Pito's eyes burned with conviction as he walked furiously over to the other side of the encampment. His nostrils flared, and he laid his head on his hands. Pito walked impatiently.

"Why isn't he talking?" said Pito.

"He's been brought back from the dead. What would you think?" said the shaman.

"I don't believe I have a nephew. We must contact Atticus," said Pito.

"First, we must pass the Kernanites and defend the Pedisax. We owe them that much. We need to go to the caves," said Captain Reno.

Captain Reno loaded a hodit, and Pito and Sicro got on the back of another one. As they left the encampment, they looked up at the massive warships hovering overhead and continued with their hodit. It was not long before they reached the caverns. A Pedisax soldier greeted them.

"There is not much time before the entire force of the Kernanites is upon us," said the warrior.

"I have an idea," said Captain Reno.

The Pedisax growled a bit but then gave him a look of curiosity. The Pedisax had been taken by surprise and remembered the generosity of Reno and everyone who had lived on Y'Fert. Captain Reno handed the Pedisax soldier a transponder.

"We'll use a transponder signal to lure the Kernanite Fleet onto one of the moons of Y'Fert. Tell your soldiers to launch this transponder at one of the low-orbiting warships," said Captain Reno.

Captain Reno went to the top of the hills where the caverns were, and the Pedisax readied a launcher. Reno looked up at the sky and heard the missile whizzing.

"Is it working?" said Captain Reno to a Pedisax soldier.

"I have not received a response from the transponder on the moon," said the soldier.

"Look, they are beginning to move away," said another soldier.

The warships began to pull away from the surface of Y'Fert and headed towards one of the moons. As they left, their lights shone brightly in the twilight. Pito and Sicro looked up with Reno as twilight turned into night and waited for the latest news.

"We need to message Atticus," said Pito.

"Agreed," said Reno.

Captain Reno went over to the Pedisax and gave them a handwritten note. The Pedisax looked bewildered as they had not witnessed what had happened with Sicro. They only nodded in agreement when Reno gave the sign for a shaman.

When the Pedisax inputted the message to Atticus, bright lights suddenly filled the sky. Captain Reno and the others held up their hands to block the light. The Pedisax hurried to their consoles.

"The warships have crashed onto the surface on one of the moons and into each other. They have destroyed themselves," said the soldier.

"Make sure to add that to the message sent to Atticus. Tell him, for the most part, we are safe," said Reno.

"What is going to happen now?" said Sicro.

"We have to tell Atticus you are alive and we are safe from the Kernanites. Hopefully, everything is going well with him," said Captain Reno.

* * *

Atticus got up from the palace floor. Aida lay next to him. She was breathing, and Atticus touched her cheeks. She moaned and sat straight up against a pillar.

"What happened, Atticus," she said.

"Ba'Gam took you. He's dead now," said Atticus.

"I'm over here, Atticus," said a voice.

"Nead!" said Atticus.

Atticus ran over to where the voice came from in the palace. He found Nead sitting down on the floor. He was using one of his hands to cover up a wounded arm.

"It is only nothing," laughed Nead.

"I need to get some medicine for you," said Atticus.

"What you need to do is do something about the Kernanites; Make them stand down," said Nead.

"I need to show them Ba'Gam's body; I need to show them that they have been defeated," said Atticus.

"Atticus, in my shawl, is a chip holding information that will help you link up with D'Er's communication array. You can transmit a message there," said Nead.

"I will," said Atticus.

Atticus looked around the palace floor and found the shawl. He took the chip and inserted it into his utility belt. He took the camera and took some video of Ba'Gam's body.

"I'm sending the video and messages to the Kernanites," said Atticus.

It only took a matter of minutes before the bombing of Craigo and the coast stopped. Atticus ran to the palace entrance and then up the cliffs toward Craigo. Kernanite warriors were taking ships up to the warships orbiting D'Er. He found a passerby and stopped him.

"Do you have any medicine with you?" said Atticus.

The stranger looked at Atticus sternly and laughed. Then he slapped him on the shoulder and gave him a medicine pouch. He smiled broadly.

"You are Atticus," said the stranger.

"Yes, I am," said Atticus.

"This war with the Kernanites did not last long. Do you know why?" the stranger said.

"We killed their leader. The threat is over now," assured Atticus.

Atticus returned to the underground palace to administer the medicine. His communicator on his utility belt began to beep, and he received the message: It was Captain Reno.

"Atticus, if you are receiving this, I wanted to let you know that we cured Pito, Sicro returned, and we have repelled the Kernanites from Y'Fert," said Captain Reno.

Atticus' eyes swelled with pride and joy. They had won the war. Atticus programmed a message for Captain Reno and the others to come to D'Er.

Atticus administered medicine to both Aida and Nead. It took about half a day for both of them to feel better. Tears were flowing from Atticus' eyes throughout the day.

Aida got up from the ground and sat on the steps leading up to the throne in the main room. Nead did the same. Atticus' communicator beeped again.

"Atticus, this is General Shor of the D'Er. What are your orders now?" said the general.

Atticus was hesitant to respond. He had never told an entire army what to do before and felt overwhelmed.

"Tell your soldiers only engage the Kernanites when necessary," said Atticus.

"Yes, sir," said the general.

"Atticus, come sit by me," said Aida softly.

"What is it?" said Atticus.

"I feel…I feel…the threat is gone," said Aida. She looked over her body, which was no longer glowing, and let out cries of joy.

"I know, it's over," said Atticus.

"We'll stay here in the palace," said Atticus.

Nead got up and looked at his wound. He bowed to Atticus and hugged him, and then he let out a victorious yell.

"Glad you returned. The people of Fina would be proud of you. Word of what has happened should be reaching them by now," said Nead.

"I'll go up to one of the villages by Craigo to gather some supplies," said Atticus.

Atticus returned to the top of the cliffs and went to a nearby village. The villagers were dancing in the streets and waving the banner of the House of D'Er everywhere. They were even burning what equipment the Kernanites had left.

"No need for this," said a villager to Atticus. He tossed a triple ion weapon into the fire. Atticus smiled as he received a warm welcome from the villagers.

"I'll have two loaves of bread, some soup, and rations," said Atticus to a street vendor.

"D'Er is lucky. One of its own came back just like the myths say," said the vendor.

"Thank you for the compliment," said Atticus. He sipped some juice while he soaked in the jubilant atmosphere. He felt the celebration would be complete with the others' return.

The night began to fall on the village, and Atticus returned down the cliffs to the ancient underground palace. He placed the food and drink on a forgotten table in the main room. Aida was now looking around the room at the various artifacts and came across the two thrones sitting side by side.

Atticus's communicator beeped, and he received a message. It was Captain Reno. He went over to Aida and hugged and kissed her.

"They're here!" said Atticus.

"Who are they?" said Nead.

"They are friends. They defeated the other Kernanite Fleet. And, they have the Chalice of Life with them," said Atticus.

"Atticus, this is Captain Reno. We are going to fly down to the surface," said Reno.

"Gotcha," said Atticus.

By the time Captain Reno and the others reached the palace, it was midnight. Wolves howled in the distance. The waves crashed on the cliffs, and the wind blew gently.

When Atticus saw Sicro, he wept with joy. He hugged them all, and he thanked the gods. A Pedisax soldier was with them.

"Atticus, we brought a Pedisax soldier with us to teach them about the outside world," said Captain Reno.

"Very well, very well, all are welcome," said Atticus.

Aida looked at Sicro's face and laughed. She hugged and kissed him until he was embarrassed. Aida knew it was her son who had come back from the dead.

"Atticus, we should get married right here, right now! Could you do it, Nead? Could you marry us?" said Atticus.

"Yes, I am one of the priests of power who can marry you," said Nead.

Aida leaped for joy and went over to the thrones. Atticus searched his coat for a piece of metal that he had wrapped around his finger to fix an ion weapon. Pito, Sicro, and Captain Reno clapped their hands.

Nead walked over and stood before the thrones. Captain Reno and the others gathered around Aida and Atticus. Atticus placed the metal ring he found in his coat on Aida's finger. The priest gave a quick blessing, and then they kissed.

"We should go up to the top of the cliffs to look out over the sea," said Aida.

"Not before we sit on the thrones," said Atticus.

Aida went over and took her seat on the left throne, and Atticus took his seat on the right. It felt right for them to sit on the thrones, and Atticus felt his parents' presence there.

At the top of the cliffs in the distance, fireworks exploded in the sky. Atticus held Aida closely, and the wind whipped around them. Atticus wanted this moment to last forever.

Captain Reno and the others reached the top of the cliffs, where they found Aida and Atticus. Pito and Sicro looked amazed at the fireworks they saw. Reno started a fire for them to sit around during the celebration.

"I'm so happy you're back, Sicro," said Atticus.

"I am as well. You did well," said Aida.

Pito coughed and went over to Captain Reno. Pito grumbled a bit, but nothing out of the ordinary. Atticus looked at Pito, who was moving away from them.

"Is everything all right?" Atticus said.

"I feel like I've been replaced since Sicro came back. It was bad enough we were separated for so long, Atticus," said Pito.

"You'll always be my brother," said Atticus.

Pito smiled and looked down at the crackling fire. The wind picked up the orange embers and tossed them over the cliffs to the sea. Night birds called to each other during the first hours of moonlight.

Captain Reno decided to make camp for everyone. Aida lay beside Atticus, and they both gazed up at the stars. A shooting star crossed the night sky, and Nead said a prayer. Sicro and Pito exchanged stories well into the night after the others had fallen asleep.

When daylight came, they all set out for a neighboring spaceport city called Woer. Woer had managed to repel attacks by the Kernanites and take in less damage. It was up in the hills towards the mountains of Craigo.

The air was crisp and clean as they went further up the hillsides. Atticus led the way, followed by Aida and Nead. Captain Reno kept a close for stragglers coming in from the Kernanites.

"So, Aida," said Captain Reno, "Where do you and Atticus plan on settling in now that the war is over?'

"Fina," said Adia.

"Oh really, the Independent Worlds need some diplomats to help them out with the mess the Kernanites and their allies left," said Captain Reno.

"No," said Aida, "Fina needs us now; the war is over. We are their children, and we owe it to them. They are our people."

"But what about Atticus? He is now from the House of D'Er, a ruler of an entire world.," said Captain Reno.

"It doesn't matter. Love is love," quipped Aida.

"Why are we going to this city?" said Captain Reno to Aida.

"Atticus needs more confirmation that this rulership is truly meant for him," said Aida.

"But, hasn't all this time, all this waiting and fighting, been enough," said Captain Reno.

"It has, and the help of friends confirmed it more. Now, he needs it from the people. Officially," said Aida.

Atticus and the other went inside the city limits of Woer. The port was bustling with trade and celebration. Atticus and the others kept to the back in the alleyways so the locals would not see them. They all went to a temple and said a prayer. The local priests congratulated Nead on his marriage of Atticus and Aida.

"Ah, well, this is not *all* for me. It's for the children of Fina. We are all children of Fina. It's for Sicro, Atticus, and Aida. And Pito and Captain Reno," said Nead.

"You all have done a mighty deed for the galaxy," said a priestess.

"Think nothing of it," said Atticus.

The priest and priestesses showered them with flowers as they left the temple. Captain Reno tried to shake them off, and so did Pito and Sicro. Aida giggled as the flower dropped across the staircase leading to the street.

"Atticus, when do you think we could return to Fina?" said Aida.

"Anytime!" said Atticus.

"I feel you're not telling me something," said Aida.

"First, I need to confirm something with an old family friend," said Atticus.

They walked three winding alleyways until they came upon a small house. The door was slightly opened. The lights in the room were candles. A book lay in the center of the room on a table.

Atticus' tattoo began to glow, and so did Aida's skin. A figure appeared at the far end of the room by the table. The figure was hooded, and Aida, Atticus, and the others went forward.

"Hello, Atticus and Aida," said the figure.

"Who are you?" said Atticus.

"I am a child of Fina, like yourself on a journey," said the figure.

My journey has ended, sir. The war is over. I found my parent's planet," said Atticus.

"Or has your journey ended," said the figure.

The figure took off his hood. It was a bright blue Humar—Aida's species. The journey had begun again.